Cynthia Blake has it all

As a successful businesswoman who owns a chain of ice cream shops in Scottsdale, Arizona, she knows life couldn't be much sweeter. But when a drunken birthday realization turns into the plan of a lifetime, Cynthia announces she'll date one man a month for the next year and marry one of them at the end of it all. In this introductory book to the Flavors of the Month series, Cynthia quickly learns just how complicated life and love can get. Has the perfect flavor been in front of her all along?

THE PLAN

FLAVORS OF THE MONTH, BOOK ONE

PENNY MCLEAN

A NineStar Press Publication
www.ninestarpress.com

The Plan

This is a work of fiction. Names, characters, places, and incidents are either the product of the author's imagination or are used fictitiously. Any resemblance to actual persons living or dead, business establishments, events, or locales is entirely coincidental.

First Edition, April 2023

ISBN: 978-1-64890-627-5

Also available in eBook, ISBN: 978-1-64890-626-8

CONTENT WARNING:
This book contains sexually explicit content, which may only be suitable for mature readers. Depictions of multiple partners and cheating

To Brittany: for your keen eye, innate nerdiness, kindness, and unfailing friendship. I dedicate this one to you because of that one scene that makes you blush.

Chapter One

December 26

Drunk and full of birthday cake: the best way to make life-altering decisions. That's my new motto. It's taken me thirty-one years to come to this realization, but all my best ideas have come this way. Probably. I don't actually have the data to back that up.

"Hey, Cyn," Kim laughs as she plunks a dollop of frosting on my nose. "Weren't you supposed to be married with three kids by now? Wasn't that *The Plan*?"

The emphasis on the last word is like a knife in my ovary. Sixteen-year-old me had been a bit cocky when she showed up at lunch one day and dropped a manifesto on the table for my two best friends to see. Simply titled *The Plan,* it outlined what I was going to do with my life and when I would do it by. This wasn't some whim. I'd really thought this shit out.

And to be fair, I hit almost every goal in *The Plan* on time or ahead of schedule. Am I the owner of a successful chain of ice cream parlors? Yup. In fact, there are currently eleven Sinfully Good locations throughout the Valley (Phoenix, that is) and Southern California. Do I own my own condo in Scottsdale and a vacation home in San Diego? Yes and yes. Am I married to the love of my life and somehow still skinny after having three of his children?

Well, I'm still skinny. Which really comes in handy for those rare getaways to the beach house. Speaking of which. *Mental note—must make time to get back to beach house.*

It turns out achieving the career parts of *The Plan* kept me a little busier than I thought it would, and no guy was ever able to keep up. There were contenders along the way and a few times when I thought I might have it all, but then the economy tanked and it took every ounce of business savvy in my five-foot-eight-inch frame to stay afloat. Lucky for me, people going through a recession tend to eat their emotions, and my flavors are incredibly soothing.

So, there I sit, hyperventilating as I try to blow out all those candles and realizing Kim has a point. In my uber-focused career path, I have completely let my love life fall to pieces. A few (read: five) celebratory shots of Fireball later, a new plan comes to mind.

"Well, for starters, I'm going to stop sleeping with Carter," I announce.

"I'll believe that when I see it," says Meg, who has a right to be skeptical.

For the past three years, I've enjoyed a friends-with-benefits arrangement with a guy I met at the gym. I blame that Justin Timberlake movie, but it really has been beneficial for us both. We've managed to keep things casual while he gets through med school and I conquer the world of dairy deliciousness. He's even one of my most trusted tasters for new flavors, but that's mostly because he likes the way the ice cream tastes on my…

Well, anyway, it doesn't matter what he eats the ice cream off, because it's going to stop. Tomorrow. I mean, a girl needs birthday sex, right? Carter was on call last night, but he said he wants to stop by tonight to say hi and, as he put it, "let me blow out one more candle." I'll have to remind him the birthday girl shouldn't be required to give a blow job, but we'll cross that bridge when we come to it.

So, yes, no more sleeping with Carter. That's obviously got to happen. The rest of the Plan still seems a bit crazy to me, but Meg and Kim seem to think it's brilliant. Let's see how it feels without a Fireball-induced fog.

1. I will date one man each month next year, starting in January.

That gives me five days to find someone on either a dating website or the old-fashioned-in-person way. Shouldn't be too hard once I tell them it has to end after thirty days. Although I probably shouldn't tell them about the next stipulation.

2. *I will marry one of the twelve men.*

Chapter Two

December 27

Okay, yes, I know it sounds a little crazy, but if people can meet on those reality shows and fall in love, why can't this work? *Note to self—look up how many of those relationships have worked out.*

So, pending some research on that topic, I feel like this is a solid plan. Out of twelve contenders, I really believe I can find a man to spend the rest of my life with. My shops are all doing well, and I've got Samantha running most of the show. True, I had planned to open a few more this year, hence why I hired her in the first place, but an investment in myself is the gift that keeps on giving.

That is cheesy. No, dammit, it's true. I've spent far too long focused on business and money and, frankly, both are in good shape at the moment. At thirty-one, I could technically retire and live comfortably on the revenue my beach house earns alone, but it'd be nice to stay in that house a bit more often rather than just take in the money. I've got it split into three apartments to rent out and always make sure to schedule myself a few days in the one-room unit in the back each year. Perhaps I'll see if one of my fellas wants to join me out there one month. Hmmm...that could be nice.

I look down at the scratch paper we jotted down my new *Plan* on and notice a barely legible title I must have added after the girls crashed in the guest room.

Flavors of the Month

Ah, a tribute to my favorite part about Sinfully Good. We always come up with a Flavor of the Month based on customer feedback from each of the stores. The customer who submits that month's flavor gets all the ice cream they can eat for a month, and we put their picture up on the wall. Sometimes we keep the flavor longer if it's a hit and I give the creator a kickback on the sales as a thank-you. Sometimes the flavors bomb, and I politely tell the customer it just doesn't mesh with that season's lineup, but to keep submitting in case they win again.

I think I'll be able to find twelve guys on my own, but maybe I should ask for some customer suggestions in that area, too, just in case. I'll keep that in my back pocket.

*

It's 6:05 when Carter walks through my door. He has a key, so I shouldn't be surprised, but he said he'd be over at 6:00, which usually means 6:30 at the earliest, and I'm walking from the bathroom to the kitchen in just a towel when I see him come in.

"Well, I was hoping you'd just be in your birthday suit, but that's close enough," he says with a tired grin. I can always tell when he's had a rough day in school because his eyes look a little droopy, but I thought they'd go easy on him in this mini-semester during winter break. I can't even believe they have classes the week between Christmas and New Year's, but I didn't go to school to save people's lives, so what do I know?

"Hey," I say as he comes close and tries to make me drop my towel. "I was just coming out here to grab my new underwear out of the laundry, young man. Hold your horses."

Oh, and did I mention Carter is twenty-six? Ha, yeah, the perfect age for a fuck buddy.

"Now what's the point of that?" His eyes begin to come alive. "I'm just going to take them off of you."

"Yes, but I'd hate to rob you of the experience," I fire back. If there's one thing Carter loves, it's taking my clothes off. He's very methodical about the whole thing and loves to take his time. Not that he's predictable, but he usually takes my panties off with his teeth and...oh, who am I kidding? I love it too.

"True, true," he sighs. "Go get dressed, birthday girl. I'll get my spanking hands warmed up."

*

I don't end up telling Carter about the Plan tonight, because really, there isn't time.

I go back to my room and decide to take my time getting ready. I mean, if it's our last time together, I want to look nice for the guy who's been so great to me these past few years.

First, I double check that I haven't missed any spots when I shaved my legs. I have, of course, missed several, so I go back over those spots and put on Carter's favorite lotion. It's really silky and smells like almonds and I'm pretty sure just one whiff gives him an erection. I don't have to worry about shaving my lady bits because I got waxed last week, but I give myself a once-over to be sure there are no errant hairs lingering.

I wasn't lying about the new underwear, and I must say they look pretty damn good. Black lace boy shorts that scrunch in the back to give my ass a little more definition (not that it needs it). I have the matching demi bra, which I don't exactly need with the dress I was planning to put on, but the thought of Carter taking it off me is enough to put it on. Plus, it gives my breasts perfect cleavage, so why not?

I'm one of those women I'd hate if I wasn't also such a nice person, if you know what I mean. Yes, I mentioned I'm skinny, but my boyish figure from high school has shifted into a shapelier look in recent years.

I put on fifteen pounds one summer in Europe while I honed my ice cream skills to perfection and came home with an hourglass look that sat well on my frame. After getting back on track with running and my usual workout routine, I dropped some of the weight (though I kept most of it in the form of muscle), but somehow managed to retain perfect 32DD boobs. Like I said, I'd hate me too.

I put my black peep toe Jimmy Choo heels on before my dress because I don't think there's anything sexier than a woman in her underwear and high heels. I already put on a tiny bit of makeup (I rarely wear much), so I give my long brown hair a quick blow-dry before deciding to leave it down and soft. I skip perfume so as not to block my almond scent and make a mental note to buy new lotion tomorrow so I'm not constantly reminded of Carter when I fuck other guys. Hmm, maybe I should buy twelve new lotions, one for each month? I like it.

I pull a casual T-shirt dress on over my head and surmise that I look just right for my last hook-up with Carter. The dress has no shape to it, but it clings to me where I want it to and has that "I look nice without even trying" vibe I'm going for.

There was a time when I thought things might develop with Carter, and Lord knows I wanted them to, but the five-year age gap felt like a lot when he was twenty-three and I was twenty-eight. I think he knew I wanted him to be my boyfriend. Okay, I know he did. When a guy blurts out, "Man, thank *God* that's not us," after I casually mentioned my friends had gotten engaged, it's a pretty strong hint he's not in it for the long haul. When he keeps making comments like that over the next week to drive the point home, you just learn to let it go.

But that's not what tonight is about. I throw some cherry ChapStick on my lips and head out to the living room. Thinking I'll find Carter on his phone, I'm a bit confused when I walk out to a candlelit space, a la the *Friends* episode where Monica and Chandler get engaged (ugh, it still makes me cry).

"I thought I'd make it special for your birthday," he says with a shy smile.

If there's one thing Carter has down, it's that smile. He's six two with short brown hair, deep-brown eyes, and the body of a swimmer. Okay, he is a swimmer, so that makes sense, but if you've seen the chest and shoulders of a swimmer, you know why I mention it. He was really nerdy in high school, so no girls noticed his looks under his baggy clothes and backward hats, so he still has no idea he's gorgeous, which has worked out great for me.

I look down at my coffee table to see he's brought wine and Skittles, which actually sounds really awful, even though I love both of those things. In fact, I hate that new Skittles have replaced lime with green apple, and I told him so, but, ah, I digress.

I grab a glass of wine from his outstretched hand and lean forward to quickly kiss him. Before I can pull away, his hand is on the small of my back pulling me toward him for a kiss I can only describe as hungry. I moan before I even realize what's going on and accidentally drop my glass of wine on the floor.

"Leave it," he says into my hair as I start to pull away.

And I do.

*

From there, things get…interesting.

Usually, Carter and I chat about our days for a bit and then just kinda go for it. If either of us is in the mood for something in particular, we're happy to vocalize it.

But tonight, there is no chitchat to be had. The hungry kiss turns into a hungry make-out session on my couch. With our lips still attached, we fall onto the cushion behind Carter and after some rearranging, I open my legs to straddle his lap. Though I can feel his hardness greet me on impact, we still just kiss, eagerly and passionately, for as long as I've ever kissed anyone.

With both of his hands in my hair keeping me pinned to his face, I realize this is probably the longest we've been in a room together before he's touched my breasts. Sometimes, he just walks into the room and puts both hands out to give them a squeeze.

Carter must realize this at the same moment I do because he pulls away from me long enough to take a peek down the front of my dress.

"Hello, girls," he whispers. "I'll get to you in just a minute."

I throw my head back to laugh and feel the eager lips from before on my neck, but softer this time. I'm in front of customers too often to have visible hickeys, and Carter is very respectful of that. Rather than suck on my skin, as I'm guessing he is dying to do based on how swollen my lips are, he plants gentle kisses all the way from my chin, down below my left ear, and across to my collarbone. From there, he pushes his head down and in between my breasts, which are rather inviting even underneath my dress.

"Well, time for this to come off." He reaches down and starts to pull my dress up and over my body.

I put my hands up to help the cause and find myself hanging for a minute as he takes his time, slowly unveiling my body to his eyes, which are now completely alert. I get an approving nod for the new underwear, and a big, breathy sigh for my navel and bra. The dress finally makes it up over my face and hands and I reach down to start unbuttoning Carter's shirt. I expect him to open my bra, but instead he caresses my face. We lock eyes for a moment before kissing again as I clumsily work the buttons through their holes. As good as Carter is at undressing me, I fear I am equally inept at taking off his clothes, but neither of us ever mentions it.

I slide his shirt over his shoulders and shimmy it down his arms so he can slip out of it. Normally, I'd press myself to his chiseled chest at this moment, but his face has once again found its way into the softness of my bosom, and I frankly can't get enough. His tongue comes out to lick in between and on top of my breasts. Even without the bra, they're perky as hell, and now his tongue is on me, they sit erect as my nipples harden.

I reach back and unclasp my bra, which irks Carter.

"Hey, now, that's my favorite part," he jokingly scolds me. "I'll have to add that to your birthday spankings."

"Maybe that's what I was hoping for."

"I'll bet you were."

Carter pulls my bra down over my arms and reacts as if he's uncovered a priceless work of art as my breasts come into full view. Before I can laugh at the look on his face, his mouth has covered as much of my left breast as he can fit into it, and I again throw my head back in sheer ecstasy. I have always, always loved everything to do with my breasts, which probably stems back to the days when I had very small boobs and every act of acknowledgment felt like I'd won the sexual lottery.

But now, oh now, I have the kind of breasts women pay thousands of dollars for, I feel so damn sexy all the time, even in my apron at work.

Carter's tongue brings my nipples to an even harder state, and I start to grind my hips on him as a wetness comes between my thighs. Knowing no customer will ever see this part of my body, he sucks and even bites all around both of my tits, not caring if he leaves marks. With my head laid back, he uses one hand to stroke up and down from my neck onto the breast he's not currently licking, and I feel desire in each of his fingertips.

Just as a barely audible "oh yes" escapes my lips, Carter grabs me around the waist and stands up. I wrap my legs tight around him as he carries me down the hall toward the bedroom. He lays me down on the bed and almost rips my panties in his attempt to get them off faster. It's not like him, but this whole night has been a little different, and I quickly forget about it when his mouth covers my lady parts.

This isn't something we normally do for two reasons: 1. I never ask for it, which I'll explain, and 2. I have other ways of taking care of my clit.

One of the best parts of having a fuck buddy is getting to ask for whatever you want. After we'd been hooking up for six months, I announced that I'd like to use my vibrator before/during sex to help me get off. Carter was all for it and said it turned him on that I was so into it. After that, we just got in the habit of relying on different toys to help me climax a few times each night, and I never asked for oral help. I mean, it's more efficient, right?

That may be true, but with Carter's tongue expertly finding my clitoris, I'm starting to wonder why I made the request in the first place. I arch my back as my clit starts to swell, and warn him if he keeps it up, I may come all over his face.

A quick nod and "hmmm" let me know he's actually hoping for that outcome, so I just lie back and enjoy. With his tongue pulsating on my clit and both hands rubbing my inner thighs, my body starts to tense up with pleasure. I mumble "fingers" and am rewarded with the index and middle finger of Carter's right hand inside me, expertly hitting spots that make the attention on my clit even more fantastic. I climax just before Carter pulls away to take a breath, and his face is dripping with my wetness as he smiles up at me.

"Get inside me," I moan, as he quickly strips off his jeans and briefs.

As he slides up on top of me, he gently kisses me, and I taste myself on his lips. I had forgotten that I taste so sweet, and I can even smell my almond lotion on his cheeks.

It's almost enough to make me come again.

*

Carter presses himself inside me and I shudder as I take him all in. I've only told Kim and Meg this before, but he has a perfect penis. It's straight and long and thick and he's great at lasting just the right amount of time before I end up sore or uncomfortable. He starts out slow and leans forward to whisper, "How does the birthday girl want it tonight?" into my ear as he picks up the rhythm a bit.

"This is great so far," I whisper back. "Go with your instincts."

Carter's instincts are to get me to climax as many times as possible, it seems. From my bedside table, he pulls out my favorite vibrator and turns it on. It's small enough to fit between us in most positions, but powerful enough to get me off a few times if I'm lucky. He locks eyes with me and places the vibrator right on my clit as he puts one hand on my hip to guide himself in and out of me. The combination is overwhelming and it's only another minute before I'm in the throes of orgasm number two.

From there, Carter drops my vibrator and again picks me up, this time with him inside me. He walks us over to the wall and puts my hands above my head as he begins thrusting from below. He holds both of my wrists with one hand and slides the other one under my ass to support me and starts bouncing me harder and harder. My tits are jostling up and down, hard, and I start to smile as I realize how damn sexy we must look right now.

Carter sees it, too, and soon his face is buried in my breasts as his hand under my ass starts to move a bit. He looks up at me for approval and I give a quick "what the hell" nod to let him know he can slide a finger inside me. I never let him fuck me in the ass because I've never liked it and his dick is too big, but he's such an ass man that I've started to let him use a finger there every now and again. He immediately moans and so do I. The added pressure combined with his thrusting cock is threatening to bring me to climax again.

Before I get there, though, we're back on the move. He brings me back to the bed, lays me on my side, and pulls my left leg up to his shoulder for easier access. He shoves himself back inside me and gives my ass a little smack.

"That's one," he says, with a devilish look in his eyes.

"Thirty more?" I ask with exaggerated eyes.

"At least," he says.

The spankings never hurt, but each sting gives me a start. He slaps my ass with each thrust, and I know he won't last long like this. He reaches over my head to find the discarded vibrator and turns it back on.

"Come for me one more time," he says, clearly determined to keep me happy tonight.

I press the vibrator down onto my clit and the stimulation is so intense I pull it off again for a few seconds while I catch my breath. His cock is throbbing and swelling and I know I don't have much time, so I push it back onto myself and my body starts to tremble with pleasure as it rises to a frenzy.

A barely audible "now" escapes his lips and we manage to both orgasm together, him exploding inside me while I contract in ecstasy and add to the sticky wetness all around us. Carter collapses in a heap beside me after slowly pulling out. He grabs a towel from my nightstand for a perfunctory clean-up, but we're both too exhausted to get up. Even though it's not even seven o'clock, I'm starting to fade and know he's going to pass out soon too.

Just as I reach over to turn out the light by the bed, his body does the "falling asleep shudder" and I shift to my side of the bed to give him some space. Feeling my absence, he rolls toward me in one last move of consciousness just as the words "I love you" fall out during an exhale.

Chapter Three

December 28

Like I said. Things got interesting. How am I supposed to explain my new *Plan* after that startling admission? Or was it even an admission? Not likely, seeing as how Carter is always the one bringing up our status and keeping it clear that he likes us just as we are. He was post-orgasm. Can't be held to anything we say during those moments, right?

But still, whether he meant it or not, Carter's not going to marry me, and that's what my new *Plan* is all about. Being loved and being fucked well is nice, but friendship is what lasts and makes a marriage great, right? Sure, Carter and I are friends, but it's easy to maintain a friendship based on booty calls and takeout. We'd never survive anything more than that.

We end up waking up around ten with growling stomachs and decide to have some dessert.

"The best thing about fucking you is you always have ice cream in your freezer," says Carter as we stumble out to the kitchen.

See? Definitely not the words of a man who's in love with me.

We each grab a bowl of our favorite flavors (I'm mint chocolate chip, Carter loves cookies n' cream, which I make with homemade Oreo-type cookies) and climb back in bed to watch Netflix.

"Thanks for the Skittles," I say during a commercial break.

"Oh, is that what we're calling your orgasms now?"

"Ha! No, but we should," I say as I lightly punch him in the arm.

"I know you hate the green apple ones," he says, "so I pulled all of them out and replaced them with the lime ones from a different bag."

Okay, that *kinda* seems like the act of someone who loves me.

*

I wake up around five the next morning and quietly slip out of bed. As I'm pulling my running shorts on over my naked ass, I hear Carter stir.

"Just using me for my body and taking off?" he says with a playful smile.

"You know it," I fire back. "Actually, thought I'd go for a run before breakfast. Care to join me?"

"What the hell." He climbs out of bed. He has morning wood and I can't help but stare for a minute. He catches me ogling and sways from side to side. "Want to work up a sweat right here instead?"

"If you can keep up with me on a five-mile run, I'll suck your cock in a post-run shower for a while," I say.

His eyebrows go up. I'm the faster runner, but I may have just given him the ultimate challenge.

"Deal. If you win, I'll fix you breakfast, serve it in bed, and take care of you however you like for dessert."

"You're on."

*

Like I said, I'm a fast runner, but it's amazing what men will do when a blow job is on the table. I jokingly told Carter once that if he did all of my laundry, I'd blow him every night for a week. My clothes were pristinely folded, hung, and put away before I got home from work the next night.

Today is no exception. I don't take it easy on him at all (breakfast in bed sounds pretty damn good), but he beats me back to the condo by about a hundred feet. Covered in sweat and panting hard, he can barely breathe as he winks at me and says, "Care to join me for a shower?"

"A deal's a deal." I shrug.

We drag ourselves up the stairs to the master bedroom and peel off our sweaty clothes. I hop in the shower first to get the water to a comfortable temperature (warm, but not scalding) and turn around to see Carter looking at me with those hungry eyes again.

He steps into the shower and joins me under the water, grabbing my body wash bottle along the way. After putting some in his hands, he begins washing my body with lingering stops at his favorite areas.

"I didn't realize my boobs were so dirty." I laugh at how long he spends washing them.

"Oh, yes, they're filthy," he says. "I'm just being thorough."

After we've both washed our bodies and hair, I look down to see Carter's dick has become fully erect. I ease my way down his body, kissing his neck, chest, and belly on the way. By the time I'm level with his cock, he's let out a moan of anticipation. "Sweet," I think to myself. "This won't take long at all."

Even though Carter lasts as long as I want him to when we fuck, I usually have no problem getting him off with my mouth. I hate to brag, but I have a really skilled tongue. It's long and somewhere along the line, I must have picked up a few tricks because I've always gotten the same reaction. I've even gotten good enough at sensing when a man is about to come that I rarely end up with any in my mouth (because ew).

I start by circling the tip of his penis with my tongue with soft, playful strokes. He's so hard I can't imagine he'll even need a minute, so I take him all the way into my mouth and add a little bit of pressure. I bring my right hand up around his shaft and begin stroking him with my hand as well as my mouth in a rhythm that starts out slow before I pick up the pace.

I feel Carter's hands in my hair as the water from the shower drips over us both. He gently guides my head back and forth to show me what feels good and as he starts to go faster, I realize we're just about done. I take him out of my mouth, look up, and smile at the face he makes when he's climaxing. I use my hands to point him right between my breasts and let his warmth cover me until I'm all sticky.

Carter's whole body shudders as I stand up and reach for my body wash.

"Looks like all that work I did to get you clean was for nothing," he says.

"No worries," I say as I wash myself off. "A deal's a deal."

Once we're both clean and we've caught our breath, I linger in the bathroom while Carter heads to the kitchen. It's Saturday and I have nothing planned, so I don't need to get myself completely put together, but I go through a quick morning routine of moisturizer, throw some product in my hair, and decide to let it air dry before throwing on my favorite pair of jeans and a tank top with a built-in bra. Honestly, it's not big enough to hold or support me, but I'll throw on a T-shirt over it if we go anywhere.

We. Why am I thinking we'll be going anywhere? I really need to tell Carter all about the new Plan and I can't imagine he'll want to hang out with me for too long after that. Besides, I need to get to work on finding my first month's guy and having Carter as my wingman doesn't seem like the best idea.

I head to the kitchen and find Carter making pancakes wearing nothing but boxer briefs and one of my frilly aprons. It's adorable, and I find myself tilting my head and smiling at him when he turns around to catch my eye.

"So, what's on the agenda today?" he says, giving me a wink. "Besides all the sex and pancakes of course."

"Well, I actually have something I want to chat with you about," I say. No time like the present, right?

"Funny, so do I," he says in a quiet voice.

We sit down at the table together to eat the pancakes he's made (to which he added strawberries and whipped cream, by the way. Seriously, why can't this man be the one?), and I get the feeling I should let Carter tell me what he has to say first. With any luck, he wants to break off our arrangement and I won't feel badly at all about sharing my news.

"I wanted to chat about our arrangement," starts Carter, who suddenly can't make eye contact with me.

I knew it. I'm a damn mind reader, it seems.

"Don't worry, Carter, you don't have to say it," I interrupt.

"I don't have to say what?" he replies, looking back up at me with an expectant expression.

"If you want out, you couldn't have picked a better time."

"Oh?" He looks a bit taken aback.

"Here's the thing. I always thought I'd be married by now and I know it's totally not what you want, and that's okay. I have loved your company and friendship and I'm not going to kid myself any longer that you are ever going to want that with me. I've decided on new course of action and I think you'll be kinda shocked to hear it, but I hope you'll support me."

Carter sits in silence for almost a solid minute, first looking at me, then gazing out of the window.

"What's this brilliant plan?" he finally asks.

"Well," I say, "I'm going to date one man every month this year. I've never really put myself out there like this before and Lord knows I haven't been on an actual date since before you and I started hooking up."

"You're just going to date a new guy every month for a year? That's the big plan?"

"Well, no, not exactly." I'm suddenly very aware of the intense look he's giving me. I mean, I seriously thought he'd be relieved. What's with the face?

"At the end of the year, I'm going to marry one of the guys," I tell him matter-of-factly.

And that's when Carter starts to laugh.

*

He laughs for quite a while. He laughs, then he stops to look at me to see if I'm serious before he starts laughing again so hard a tear rolls down his cheek. I'm about to tell him he's being an asshole when he says, "Sorry, sorry. I shouldn't be such an asshole."

Okay, he was the mind reader on that one.

"But seriously, Cyn." He takes a big deep breath to clear the giggles. "How do you ever expect it to work?"

"Are you saying no one would want to marry me?" I seethe.

"No, no, that's not it," he says sincerely. "I just need more details, I guess. Are you going to tell these men you'd like to marry one of them after the year is over? What if you really like one of them? You're just going to dump them at the end of the month and move on, hoping they wait around?"

Shit. These are things I hadn't thought about.

"Weeeeeellll, yes. Yes, that's exactly what I'm saying. If he's the right guy, he'll wait for me."

"What if you meet the right guy in January? You think he'll love waiting for you to fuck eleven other guys until he can propose?"

Double shit. Why do I have to have such a smart fuck buddy? I should have hooked up with that hot guy who works at the movie rental place. Hot as hell, but dumber than rocks. He'd think this plan is brilliant, but he also thinks vending machines are brilliant.

"Okay, so maybe I haven't worked out all of the details, but I do know I want to focus on finding the right person and stop wasting my time on the wrong one," I throw back.

This works better than I meant it to. I just wanted Carter to stop looking at me like I'm an idiot. Instead, he is now looking at me like I kicked his dog in the face. He stands there considering me for a while, and I think I should maybe apologize and clarify what I meant when he just nods.

"You're right," he says. "It's a weird plan, but you've always done things your own way. I support you and I hope you find what you are looking for. Heck, I'll even help you find the guy if I can. I sure as hell don't want you bringing some asshole around to give all the good ice cream to."

"Thanks, Carter. It really means a lot to me. You know me better than most people, so if you do know of anyone who you think I might like, please do send them my way."

"You got it, babe. Can I ask for a favor though?"

"Sure." It's really the least I can do, after all.

"Can I be your date for New Year's Eve? Let me be the last guy you're with before your year-long marriage hunt begins."

"I think that sounds fantastic," I say.

And I really do.

*

After Carter leaves (he says he has to get back to the library to study, but it feels like an excuse to me), I sit down and start hashing out the details of the Plan. Kim and Meg have both sent me texts with guys they think might make great first options, along with equally snarky "are you really sure you want to go through with this?" messages, and I think one of their suggestions will be the best option. I've done the online dating thing before, but a recommendation from a friend feels like a good way to kick this off. Plus, with only three days until January, I don't really have time to be sorting through a bunch of profiles online right now. I'll save that for the months when I have more prep time.

Kim has sent me a picture of a guy named Javier who she works with. She's a teacher, so odds are he is, too, and I think that could be a good possibility. I've always had a thing for teachers, probably because I was such a goody-goody growing up, and very likely because I slept with a few of my professors in college. Come to think of it, it's probably that second thing.

Anyway, Javier looks very nice. He's Hispanic and tall (he's standing next to Kim in the picture, towering over her five five frame) and has a nice smile. Her note says this:

> *I almost don't want to give you this guy yet because I think you could be really great together and maybe he should be Mr. December or something, but he's single now and not the kind of guy you should wait for. Super smart, funny, coaches the soccer team, and loves his family. If not for the whole "I love my job and it's frowned upon to date coworkers" thing, I'd go for him myself.*

So, there you have it—a solid recommendation from a friend about a good-looking guy.

Meg has gone a different way, and I'm very torn. She sent me a picture of a guy who I'm going to call anti-Javier. Where Javier looks wholesome and sweet, Meg's friend Ken looks like a bit of a bad boy. I hate to judge by a picture, but he is covered in tattoos and straddling a Harley. I mean, he's certainly hot, but she knows I'm terrified of motorcycles. However, thanks to Adam Levine, I have developed quite the love of tattoos. Her note is hilarious.

> *Stop focusing on the damn Harley and look at his arms. Yes, he rides a bike, but he's part of one of those motorcycle gangs that does charity work with kids around town. Look it up. He's sexy and a good guy. Good luck finding that elsewhere. Fred knows him from college, and he just moved back to town, so you've got dibs. Get on it.*

Fred is Meg's fiancé, and they are getting married in February. Come to think of it, I think that helps me settle the order. I'll go for Javier in January (gotta love the J's) and Ken in February so he can be my date to Meg's wedding. That way he'll know other people there and it won't be super awkward since I'm in the wedding and everything.

So, now that I have the first two months lined up in terms of the "who," I just need to figure out the "how." I mean, how am I honestly going to tell these guys about what I have planned for them? I can hear

Carter's voice in my head and the whole thing sounds even more ridiculous now I have to put it into action.

I mess around on Facebook for a while to avoid thinking about the Plan and see a blog one of my friends posted about how to live a greener life for the New Year. I click on it (who doesn't want to be greener, right?) and it hits me: I should start a blog.

Maybe if I explain my situation clearly in writing and send it to the potential guys, it will help them understand. At the very least, it will save me several awkward conversations and if a guy isn't into it, they can politely say "no thanks" rather than having to tell me to my face. This means they'll have to be okay with being a part of a public website, but honestly, how many people could possibly want to read this? And it's not like I'll use their real names, so no harm, no foul, right?

Besides, for the one I do end up marrying, this will make for a fun way to immortalize our love story. Yes. I am officially a genius.

Chapter Four

December 29

Blogs are hard.

Like, stupid hard.

Okay, not the creating of the blog itself, but the actual writing has been really hard. Everything I write sounds *so* cheesy I can hardly stand it.

On the bright side, it looks great. I've designed it with lots of pretty ice cream cones all around and found a great font for the title bar. *Flavors of the Month* sits across the top in big, bold letters with a tagline I think is pretty perfect.

One woman's search for her forever flavor.

I added a picture of myself from a recent trip to San Diego. I'm not wearing makeup and I'm smiling at Meg, who was just off-camera, so I have a fun and carefree look going on. It's the part where I try to explain the Plan that has me stuck.

I've tried to be cute:

Could you be the mint to my chocolate chip?

Nope.

I've tried to be romantic:

I love long walks on the beach. Just looking for someone to hold my hand along the way...

Double nope.

I've tried about twenty different drafts and they all just seem wrong. I call Kim for help and her advice is annoyingly simple.

"Just write a few sentences to explain the Plan. Don't dress it up. Let them decide if they're cool with it."

Not sure why I didn't think of that, but here goes:

I am 31 and would like to spend this year focusing on finding a partner for life. I'm hoping to date one man every month this year, for that month only, and at the end of the year, my plan is to marry one of them. I am not a hopeless romantic and I am not a crazy person. I'm just a woman who spent too much time focusing on her career and not enough time on her love life. That ends now.

Well now, that's a bit short, isn't it? Should I maybe add some flair and a few...

No, Kim is right. Get to the point and write more when you have more to say, Cyn. This isn't a personal ad. It's just the introduction to a page where I can document this crazy journey I'm about to embark on. And crazy it is.

I send the link to my blog to Javier.

Shit just got real.

Chapter Five

December 30

I got a note from Carter last night asking if I was really serious. I said that I was and didn't hear back until today when he sends me a text.

> **Carter:** *How are you finding the guys? I think I might have someone for you.*
>
> **Me:** *I've got a potential January and February lined up. Is your guy available for March or after?*
>
> **Carter:** *Should be. Check in with me as it gets closer if you're still doing this. PS Wear something sexy tomorrow night.*
>
> **Me:** *Duh. It's NYE and our last date. Hope you get some rest and eat*

a good meal before we go out. You'll need your strength.

Carter: *Have mercy.*

So, somehow within three days, I have managed to line up my first three months, or at least I have leads for the first three months anyway. Javier wrote back to Kim that he was intrigued, though slightly concerned about being the first guy. Luckily for me, his New Year's resolution was to try new things and she said he'll be calling me today.

Meg liked my idea of saving Ken until February, so she sent him the link. Ken is apparently always down for trying new things and has already sent me a text.

Ken: *Hey Cynthia—this is Ken. Guess I'll be your Valentine? Fun idea. Talk to you in a month.*

I hadn't even considered that Mr. February would also be my Valentine, but I guess it makes up for the fact he gets a short month. Plus, from the look of Ken, he's more of a fling than marriage material, so getting the short month is probably perfect. And hey, who says I can't have a little fun along the way?

I promised Carter I'd wear something sexy for our NYE date tomorrow night, which wouldn't be a problem if I wanted to wear something he's seen before. Over the years, we've been each other's dates for countless functions, so he's pretty much seen all my cocktail dresses. I know he has a few favorites in the bunch, but I feel like being especially sparkly this time around.

As I head out of the door to go shopping for something new, my phone rings with a number I don't recognize. I pick it up as I throw on my sunglasses and immediately get a thrill when I hear the voice on the other end.

"Cynthia?" the voice says with an accent so thick my knees start to shake.

"This is she," I say.

"Hi, this is Javier. Kim's friend," he says.

Um, so, one thing is clear. I could tell from the picture he is Hispanic, but now, based on the voice, I am 100 percent sure he is from Spain. He speaks with a lisp that is common in some regions of the country. It's a sound that shouldn't be sexy, but somehow totally is. He sounds like a cross between Antonio Banderas in *The Mask of Zorro* and… Wait, you know what? That's exactly what he sounds like.

"Hi, Javier," I stammer. "How are you?"

"I'm very well, thank you. I was calling to see if I can take you out for the New Year tomorrow night. Or am I supposed to wait until January the first?"

He sounds like he's trying not to laugh, but that's okay. The whole thing is a little silly, but he was okay with the idea enough to call me, so I'm going to assume we're okay.

"I actually have plans with friends tomorrow night," I say, "but I'd love to see you after that if you're free."

"That's too bad. I was hoping to be your New Year's kiss. But I suppose I have thirty-one days to get to know you after that?"

Seriously. That voice. I consider bailing on Carter, but three years of loyal friend-banging makes me pause.

"That really does sound lovely, but I can't cancel on my friends."

"Of course not," says Javier. "I wouldn't want that at all. May I take you to dinner on Friday night?"

"That would be great," I say.

"I'll pick you up at eight. And Cynthia, I am looking forward to meeting you."

"Same here, Javier," I say as I hang up.

Yes. This plan was a brilliant idea.

Chapter Six

December 31

I had pretty good luck shopping yesterday and found the perfect dress for my last date with Carter. The dress is silver and so short I seriously can't sit down all night, but we're going dancing at a club that will have passed appetizers, so sitting shouldn't really be an issue anyway. I was considering new underwear for the occasion, but then I thought it might be fun to go commando and let Carter know at some point.

The dress is low cut in front and back, so a bra won't work. I opt for double-sided tape instead and figure I'll just let the girls go free for the evening. Combine that with my favorite Manolo Blahnik silver heels and I'd say I'm pretty Carrie Bradshaw, circa Season One. I throw on some fake eyelashes and more makeup than I usually apply, step back, and assess myself in the mirror.

I've just finished adding my signature almond-scented lotion to my legs when I look up and catch Carter checking me out from behind. I didn't hear him come in and I'm not sure how long he's been there, but I do know my little no-underwear secret has been ruined.

I lock eyes with Carter in the mirror and wink. I've got one leg up on my vanity chair and know I'm completely exposed. He looks down at me and sighs, then looks me back in the eye and says, "We're going to be late to the party. Don't move."

I'm about to protest that we'll mess up my hair if we move to the bed, but before I can say anything, Carter is right behind me and has pressed himself up to my exposed crotch. He's already getting hard, and I decide to just go with it. Can't blame the guy for walking in on a sight like this after all, can I?

I put my foot back on the ground and lean forward to give him a better view. He lifts my dress a little to bring my area into full view and drops to his knees. He kisses me gently and breathes me in eagerly and soon his tongue meets my wetness completely. I moan and he stands back up. He presses his cock between my legs, achingly close to where we both want it.

"We'll consider this round one," he says, spanking my ass with his hands lightly. "That's for being a bad girl and forgetting your panties." He laughs. "And don't worry. I won't mess up your hair."

God, he's really pretty perfect, isn't he? I'm about to say so when he thrusts inside me and I forget about everything else for a moment. He's got his hands on my hips and he's pulling me back into him as he pushes into me, and everything just feels so warm and so right I almost want to cry. I'm really going to miss this.

His hands reach up my dress until they find my breasts and my perfect taping job is ruined as he pulls them out from inside the dress.

"Whoops—guess we'll have to fix that," he says, with no hint of apology. Instead, he squeezes my tits a little harder with each thrust, twisting my nipples gently in his fingertips. That stimulation and the angle he's fucking me from brings me to a quick, shuddering climax. I clamp down on his dick as it happens and that's enough to bring him to join me. We stand there for a second with him resting inside me, both of us assessing the sexy reflection in the mirror.

"Will there be a round two?" I ask, coyly.

"Abso-fucking-lutely," he sighs.

*

We arrive at the club twenty minutes after Meg and Kim, but that's perfect because they're still waiting to get in. I decided not to retape my breasts to my dress, but they should stay put. They're a bit red and swollen from our pre-date fuck session and Kim giggles as she makes out what is clearly a hand mark on one.

"Kicked off your last date with a bang, did ya?" she says.

"Oh hush," I say.

"I just hope that fades before Javier picks you up tomorrow night," she whispers.

I laugh, but then it hits me. If I'm only dating this guy for thirty-one days, will he expect me to sleep with him on the first date? I never do that, but for such a short period of time, will these men expect it? I look down at my tits and realize one still has a hickey from my birthday and think I'd better at least wait until the second date...or keep the lights low for the first time.

We get into the club and grab a drink at the bar. I get the feeling Carter is preoccupied because he orders a shot instead of a full drink, slams it, and immediately takes another. Must have been a hard day of studying.

We all hit the dance floor. Meg and Fred are really good dancers, so I try to stay as far away from them as possible so as not to be judged by comparison. Kim's date is a guy named Alex, who she's been dating for a while. He's lanky and awkward and I look like a pro next to him, so that's where I stay.

Carter has been all over me since we got here, which is nice. The DJ has thrown in a few slow songs and each time one has played, Carter has pulled me close, his eyes darting around and daring anyone else to cut in. It's a bit intense, but he's been drinking and I don't think anything of it.

Later, an old-school favorite of ours comes on. "Pony" by

Ginuwine always reminds me of high school when I first learned grinding my ass into a guy was likely to be met with something hard poking me back. I felt powerful and nervous back then but have dropped the nerves and used that ploy as some sort of modern-day mating ritual ever since.

I back myself up into Carter and immediately feel him sigh. He leans down and whispers into my ear, "Careful now, or round two is going to happen in front of an audience."

"Maybe that's what I want," I laugh back.

It's really dark in the club and we're surrounded by people, so even though I know Carter won't actually fuck me right here and now, I'm somehow not surprised when he slides his fingers under my skirt in between my thighs. I lean my head back on his chest and put my hands down on my sides to block others from seeing where his hands now are, and he pushes two of his fingers up inside me. He uses his other hand on my stomach to hold me close and fingers me to the deep bass rhythm. As the song ends, he loudly announces that he needs another drink, takes my hand, and leads me off the dance floor.

It's about eleven now and nearly impossible to get to the bar, but we walk right past it toward a bank of elevators in the back. I assume we're heading up to the smaller bar on the second floor, so I don't question it when we get in. I am confused, however, when Carter pushes the button for the seventh floor, which is part of the hotel.

Sensing my gaze on him, he smiles and says, "You'll see."

We exit the elevator and head down a hallway full of hotel rooms. Various moans and music greet us from inside some of the rooms and it's obvious that New Year's Eve makes everyone a little randy.

We reach a room at the end of the hall and Carter produces a key from his pocket.

As we step through the threshold, I catch my breath at the sight of a floor-to-ceiling window with a view of the whole Valley.

"Since it's our last night together, I thought I'd go all out," says Carter, smiling at me as I take in the view.

"I love it," I say. "It's perfect. Thank you."

"You're welcome. I've been thinking a lot about your plan, and I'll admit, I was a bit upset at first."

"Upset?" I interrupt.

"Yes, but I'm not anymore," he continues. "I think it's a great idea. And for our last night together, before you embark on this journey, I'm not going to fuck you."

"I, uh, what?" I stammer.

"You heard me."

"Then why are we here?"

"I'm going to make love to you."

*

What did he just say? I'm about to voice this very question when his lips are on mine with a sudden fierce passion and there are no words to ask.

And he's right. What we do next simply cannot be considered fucking. A tenderness radiates from Carter's fingertips, and before I can even catch my breath from the kiss, he has eased me out of my dress. I am standing in front of him wearing nothing but my silver high heels, and he takes a step back to look me up and down.

"You're beautiful," he says.

I blush from head to toe and watch as he unbuttons his shirt. I press myself to his bare chest and listen to his heartbeat for thirty seconds or so. He gently lifts me off my feet and carries me to the bed.

"Roll over," he says, and I oblige, thinking this is where the fucking may begin. Instead, he begins to massage my back and shoulders, kissing the back of my neck along the way. He caresses my whole body, leaving me covered with goose bumps, then rolls me back over and takes me into his arms.

We kiss until my lips are numb and Carter stands to take his pants off. He slowly lowers himself back on top of me and enters me with one slow, deliberate thrust. I arch my back and welcome him inside. We have no toys and have done without our normal pre-sex foreplay, but my whole body is alive with anticipation of what will come next. It is neither our craziest nor our longest session, but I soon find myself in the middle of an intense orgasm that brings a tear to my eye.

Carter kisses me tenderly and wipes the tear from my face. "Did you want me to stop?" he asks with concern.

"Not at all," I say. "I must have something in my eye."

"Ahh yes, that must be it," he laughs. He reaches his hand down to my clitoris and begins stimulating me with his thumb. "Come again for me. Come with me."

With my whole body on edge and his expert maneuvering, it's not long before I do just as he asks and with one final thrust, we both collapse in a heap on the bed.

*

I must have fallen asleep because when I look at the clock, it's 11:56. Carter is dressed and smiling down at me.

"You shared your plan with me and now it's time for me to share something with you. Don't say anything because I've made up my mind and it's almost midnight. I love you, Cynthia. I've loved you for a long time and I think I was just scared to say it. I think you are everything I want in a woman, but I understand if you need to be sure. I have a year left of school and you have this plan to focus on, so let me offer you this challenge: Use the year to see if you can find someone better for you than me. If you do, I'll walk away with no hard feelings because I just want you to be happy. If you don't, I'll meet you right back here one year from today and put a ring on you so fast it'll make your head spin. I don't want to move forward with you knowing you'll always be wondering if there might have been someone better. I know January belongs to some other guy, so I'm going to kiss you one more time and walk away before next year starts, but I'm always here for you if you need to talk about anything. Get some sleep now. The room is paid for, I left clothes for you to change into in the bathroom, and breakfast is on me too. Remember, if one of these guys is better for you than me, I won't fight. I love you, and your happiness is all that matters to me. Happy New Year, babe."

Holy. Fucking. Shit.

Chapter Seven

www.flavorsofthemonth.bloggerific.com

One woman's search for her perfect flavor.

ABOUT:

I am 31 and would like to spend the year focusing on finding a partner for life. I'm hoping to date one man every month this year, for that month only, and at the end of the year, my plan is to marry one of them. I am not a hopeless romantic and I am not a crazy person. I'm just a woman who spent too much time focusing on her career and not enough time on her love life. That ends now.

JANUARY 1

Welcome to what is either the greatest or worst idea of my life. Today, and for the rest of this year, I am putting the same amount of dedication and consideration into my love life as I have always done with my career. I'm not sure yet if the heart works that way, but let's find out together, shall we?

I've loved building up Sinfully Good over the past decade and I'm so thankful to the communities who have supported our little chain of ice cream stores through the years. In a way, you all have inspired this little endeavor, as I've always enjoyed the Flavor of the Month suggestions you send me. If it can work for ice cream, perhaps it can work for love?

Okay, I feel silly for even saying that now, but since my only subscribers to this site are my two best friends, I suppose I don't need to worry about being embarrassed.

For this first month, I have been set up with a man who I will refer to as J on this site to protect his identity on the off chance this blog is ever read by others. J and I have a date planned for tonight and I am excited to meet him.

JANUARY 1

It is literally taking everything in me to not run after Carter. That, or I am still in shock. Honestly, it's probably the latter. And by literally, I mean figuratively, which is apparently an acceptable way to use the word literally now. That actually bothers me. What a weird thing to be thinking about right now.

I stumbled to my feet as soon as he left and tried to get dressed, but then I hesitated and sat back down. Nodding determinedly, I jumped up and put my dress on over my head, but then felt a bit woozy, and as I tried to sit on the bed again, I slid off the edge.

So, now I am sitting on the floor with my dress all askew, wondering what in the hell just happened. Well, technically I know what just happened, so I guess I'm really here trying to figure out how I feel about it. I mean, I have to abandon the Plan, right? The guy who I've spent the last several years in a pseudo-relationship with just told me he loves me and wants to be with me. Game over, right?

But wait—he just told me to go forward with the Plan. Why on Earth would he say that if he were so sure of me? Can he really be so selfless to stand by and watch me date twelve other guys, and just wait to see if I'll choose him at the end?

Eesh—it just occurred to me that's exactly what I'm wanting every guy to do this year.

I think…I think…I think I'm too drunk to think this through.

*

I wasn't sure if the first waffle I ordered from Room Service would soak up all the alcohol and insanity rolling around in my body, so I order a second one, just to be sure. I'm starting to feel sober and hydrated as I throw back another bottle of absurdly expensive hotel room water, but sane would not be the word I'd use to describe my current mental state. I keep replaying Carter's words inside my head, and I can't help but wonder if I'm being tested. Does he want me to call everything off to prove my love for him? Or does he have doubts of his own and needs the year to be sure of me too?

I realize that conjecture in the age of instant communication is just plain silly and decide to go straight to the source. Carter is working right now, so I figure a quick text message is something he can respond to when he has time. Plus, I'm obviously a big, scared chicken.

> ***Me:*** *So, what would you say if I called off the Plan right now and said you and I should make a go of this?*

I assume it will take him a while to answer and it's about time for me to check out of this hotel, so I make my way into the bathroom for a quick shower. I see a Target bag on the counter in the bathroom and assume it's the clothes Carter left for me so I wouldn't have to walk around in last night's dress. I'd say that's a solid checkmark under the "reasons why I should probably be with Carter" column heading.

And really, I can picture it in my head so clearly. I can plan our wedding while Carter finishes up school. He's already said he wants to stay in Arizona, so I don't have to worry about relocating. Haven't I already imagined us together more times than I can count? I can't think of anyone who knows me or *gets* me the way he does.

I step out of the shower and catch a glimpse of myself in the mirror as I dry off. I have a goofy smile on my face and last night's makeup running down my eyes and cheeks. I look like a creepy clown doll, a thought that makes me laugh so hard I almost don't hear my phone ping with a new text message.

Carter: *Call me*

Well, this is it. He's on the same page and was just making sure I felt the same way. I'll have to cancel on Javier tonight, but I doubt he'll have any trouble finding a nice girl if he's as amazing as I've been told. I reach into the Target bag and pull out a comfy pair of pink and gray yoga pants and realize Carter even knows exactly what I'd want to wear on a morning like this. Then I pull out the granny panties he bought me and make a mental note to kick him for that little prank. He's also thrown in a nice sports bra (maybe I won't kick him) and a plain white T-shirt on which he has written "Walk of Shame" in black Sharpie (definitely kicking him). I grab my phone to call him and laugh at my reflection. Luckily, the last thing in the bag is a scrunchie (kick him I must) and oversized sunglasses to hide my mess of a face (won't kick him too hard).

"Hey," he says as he answers my call.

"Hey," I reply, wondering if this important a conversation should have been done in person. I mean, we're kind of getting engaged, aren't we?

"Listen," he says, before I can finish mentally designing my dream wedding dress. "If you'd never come up with this plan, I would agree we should give us a try. I've been thinking about it for a long time, actually."

"Why does the plan change your mind?"

"Well, to be honest, I kinda thought when you were ready to settle down, I'd be the obvious choice. I was hurt and thought about just walking away, but you're too important to me to give up on. I'm glad you're feeling like maybe I could be the one now, but I couldn't marry you and always wonder if you were just settling for me because I was convenient. I don't know how I'm going to feel watching you date different guys each month, but I stand by what I said last night."

A sound fills the room, and I realize it's all the air leaving my body. Can a figurative punch in the gut really knock the wind out of you?

"However," he goes on, giving me reason to suck back in some of that air, "I think I've come up with a compromise."

"What kind of compromise?"

"I have a month between school and clinicals this year. Can I reserve the month of June?"

He wants to be one of the guys? I suddenly can't decide if this is a brilliant or terrible idea. Brilliant, right? It'll give us a chance to focus on each other and see if this is what we want. Or will it confuse everything? I should probably talk again before he thinks I've hung up or passed out.

"June. Yes. You can have June," I say.

"Great, Cyn. I think that's what's best. Now, march proudly out of that hotel wearing your fancy new clothes and let me get back to work. I'm very busy and important."

He's laughing and I should be, too, but I'm still a bit dazed. I probably shouldn't let on that I'm disappointed and borderline devastated.

"Oh yes, remind me to kick you when I see you," I say with a terribly forced laugh.

"You okay?" Of course he can hear the insincerity in my laugh.

"Oh yeah, I'm fine. Just hungover and tired and questioning my whole life. You know, the usual."

"Don't overthink it, Cyn. If it's supposed to be you and me, we'll know it a year from now."

*

Okay. Okay. No wedding with Carter to plan, so I might as well get ready to date someone new for the first time in five years. I can do this. Yup, yup, yup. Sure can.

I mean, I did see the perfect dress on *Say Yes to the Dress* last week, and that kinda feels like a sign, but…

No. Stop it, Cyn. It's time to focus on Javier. And really, what woman wouldn't kill for this kind of problem? I've got a man who loves me who is willing to wait to find out if he's my perfect guy and I have a date tonight with a sexy Spanish teacher who comes with a great recommendation from a trusted friend. I swear, if I wasn't me, I'd probably hate me for whining about this.

So now I suppose I should get ready for tonight's date. I've got six hours until Javier is supposed to pick me up, so I call and make an appointment to have my hair blown out and makeup done. I want to make a good first impression, and, really, it's just more fun to have someone else help me primp. With so much time to kill, I plop down on the couch and channel surf a bit to try to take my mind off the tumultuous last twenty-four hours and pre-date jitters.

As I reach the movie channels, I hit the jackpot—*Bridget Jones's Diary*. Will there ever be a day when I don't feel like watching this movie? Spoiler alert: no, there will not.

As I settle into the familiar pace of a movie I've probably watched about a hundred times, I make a mental note to go for whichever guy this year is the Mark Darcy-est; someone who likes me just as I am. I need the mental fortitude to steer clear of the Daniel Cleavers (or just have fun with them, but not get attached) and only give my heart away to the kind of man who can make my tummy flip the way Colin Firth does in this movie.

As I get to my absolute favorite moment of the movie—you know, the part where Bridget says nice guys don't kiss like this and Mark says, "Oh yes we fucking do"—the tension in my shoulders unwinds and I smile to myself. Stressing over all this really defeats the purpose. It's time to have some fun. And, you know, make the biggest decision of my life.

*

I am shaking with anticipation as I pace around my house and wait for Javier to show up. Or perhaps it's because I tried to calm my nerves by taking a shot of Fireball on an empty stomach. Whatever the reason, I'm shaking like a leaf and almost scream when I hear a knock on the door.

I give myself a last look in the mirror and decide I've hit the right first date look I was aiming for. My hair is down and soft and my makeup is subtle with slightly exaggerated eyes. I wasn't sure where we are going, so I settled on a plain gray dress I can dress up or down depending on the shoes I throw on as we are leaving.

"Okay, Cyn. Try not to fuck this up," I say aloud to my reflection. "It's only the rest of your life."

I walk to the door and take one more deep breath before opening it. And there he is. Javier, Mr. January, in all his glory. And glorious he is, with his black hair and dark eyes. I'd almost be able to stop right there and melt, but then he smiles and reveals the hint of a dimple in his left cheek and my knees threaten to buckle. His shirt isn't form-fitting, but I can tell there is one fit body underneath his dress shirt and jeans. I'm wondering just how fit it is when I realize he has said something and I've missed it. Shit.

He catches my face and says again, "Well hello, Cynthia. You are even more beautiful than your picture."

I blush and step forward to greet him with a… Oh crap. Do I hug him? Shake his hand? I've waited a second too long and end up reaching forward with my hand as I take a second step and accidentally graze his crotch just as he kisses me on the cheek. He deftly grabs my hand and holds it as he kisses my other cheek and pretends I didn't just grope him within ten seconds of meeting him, putting me at ease. I can feel the warmth on my cheeks where his lips were and that feeling rushes over the rest of my body as I stand awkwardly about two inches from Javier's face.

"Uh, hi, er, I mean, yes, *soy* Cynthia," I say.

Oh my God. I did not just say "soy Cynthia" in terrible Spanish, did I? I did. I freaking did. I take a step backward, ready to sneak back into my house and start this whole thing over.

But Javier just laughs and says, "Good thing we have a month to work on your Spanish. Did Kim tell you I teach Spanish at her school?"

And from there, we relax into an easy conversation as I show him into my house and offer him a drink before we head out. He politely declines, which is convenient because I'm not actually sure what I would have given him.

"So, where are we headed?" I finally ask, realizing I am still barefoot and eager to get this date going.

"I made reservations at Rick's Cafe, if that's all right with you."

"That sounds perfect." Rick's is small and romantic with great food, a perfect place to sit for a while and get to know each other.

"Wonderful," says Javier. "Shall we?"

He smiles and reaches for my hand. There's that dimple again.

Oh yes. Yes, we shall.

Chapter Eight

www.flavorsofthemonth.bloggerific.com

Had my first date with J last night and have to seriously pat myself on the back for this wonderful plan but am now concerned I am setting the bar too high to begin with. From the moment I met J, I felt a connection immediately. I had butterflies but felt at ease all at the same time. What did Carrie Bradshaw call that feeling when she met Jack Berger? Zsa zsa zu? Well, J and I have that.

I don't mean to be arrogant and assume he feels the same way, but unless he's one hell of an actor, the connection was mutual. We went to dinner at Rick's Café and had a lovely meal, followed by drinks in the lounge. J is from Spain, and even though our childhoods were obviously very different, we found we have plenty in common and lots to talk about. It was one of those nights you hope will go on forever but seems to end far too soon. But, since we have our next date scheduled for tonight, I suppose I can stand the wait until we see each other again.

JANUARY 2

I woke up this morning with so many wonderful thoughts swirling around my head and figured I'd better get the first date blog post out of the way before starting my day. Everything I wrote on there is true, but let's just say I'm leaving the best details off the internet and keeping them all to myself. Because. Oh. My. Goodness. Javier is amazing and I can't stop smiling.

I fire off a quick text to Kim (*THANK YOU THANK YOU THANK YOU*) and get ready to go for a run. As I'm tying my shoes, my phone rings. Kim, of course.

"Um, if you think you can get away with just a thank-you text and not give me details, you crazy, girl," she practically shrieks into my ear.

"I was just going for a run," I start to say.

"Fuck running," she interrupts. "I'm on my way over with bagels and Starbucks. And you are going to tell me everything."

Like hell I am, I laugh to myself. I mean, I'll tell Kim *most* of the evening, but some images are best left to my head.

I'll tell her all about dinner. I'll tell her how Javier looked me in the eye as I told him about my life, nodding, smiling, laughing, and appearing concerned in all the right places. I was equally engrossed in his story, especially as he told me about how he came to Arizona in the first place (on a scholarship to play soccer at Arizona State University) but decided to stay after falling in love with the desert. That's a big plus for me, as I have a special love for my home state.

From there, the conversation switched gears to the Plan and how he's at a similar place in his life, ready to settle down. Javier was close to being married before, but his fiancée cheated on him with his best friend a few years back and he's just now gotten over it. Trust me—the Mark Darcy similarity did not escape me.

We shared a bottle of wine in Rick's lounge area and soon found ourselves a bit tipsy and a bit snuggly. We sat in a cozy booth and listened to the piano player until the conversation hit a short lull. It wasn't that we ran out of things to say, but as we both stopped for a second to catch our breath, I realized our bodies had easily melded together and I could feel Javier's breath on my shoulder. I turned my head slightly and caught him looking down at my body, his gaze admiring. I'd opted to not wear a low-cut dress, but even still, from his angle, he would have had a great view of my ample cleavage and he didn't seem to mind.

He looked up and our eyes met for about three seconds before

Javier put his hand gently behind my head and pulled me close for a quick but eager kiss.

"We should get out of here before I do things a gentleman shouldn't do in a public place," he whispered.

"I'd kinda like to know what that entails," I whispered back, teasingly. I'd barely gotten the words out of my mouth when his other hand slid up my skirt between my legs to give my thigh a little squeeze before he stopped himself and kissed my collarbone.

"May I show you back at your place?"

Um, yes. Yes, you may, is what I thought, but instead, I just nodded.

After a short Uber ride, where we made out like teenagers, back to my place, we picked up where we left off on my couch. We kissed and explored each other's bodies with our hands, eagerly but each with some reservations. We finally pulled apart and I laughed at our situation, as Javier's hand rested on my right breast in between my dress and bra.

"I'm not sure what to do," I confessed. "I normally would say we should cool it for the night and save something for the next few dates—"

"But we only have a month and you'd rather not waste any time?" Javier sounded hopeful.

"Exactly."

"I had the same concerns. I don't want you to get the wrong idea about me, as I am as attracted to you personally as I am physically. We could wait. Maybe we should wait."

"But I don't want to wait." This time I finished his thought for him.

"Oh, thank God."

*

And that's as much of the story as I tell Kim, happy to share that, yes, we "did it." We eat and chat, and I give her the *Reader's Digest* version before she leaves. And yes, it was great. But just how great it was is something I still can't believe.

*

After we decide we both want to go all the way, I stand up and lead Javier to my bedroom. Then, and only then, do I start to feel a bit nervous about actually having sex with someone new. My room has been Carter's territory for years now. What if Javier and I aren't as compatible as I think we'll be? I hesitate for just a minute at the doorway and Javier bumps into me from behind. I'm aware of his body and his erection against me and let our bodies melt into each other for a second longer.

Soon, his hands come up around me, starting at my stomach. He holds me, firmly, and presses himself into me again from behind so I feel his urgency. I lean my head back onto his shoulder as he lowers his lips down to mine, kissing me there, then on my cheek, then onto my neck as his hands work their way up to my breasts. We walk toward the bed, still connected, and he brings his hand to my back to unzip my dress, slowly, almost painfully so.

I start to wiggle out of it and hear Javier whisper, "Patience, *mi amor*."

Oh, for fuck's sake, that accent is enough to make me wet. How can he expect me to wait?

But wait, I do, as he slowly slides my dress off my right arm, then my left. He eases it off my body, kissing my back all the way down until his face is just above the lacy thong I had so hoped he would see last night. My dress is at my feet and I kick it away as Javier stands back up and turns me to face him. I am barefoot in my matching bra and panties, and he steps back to take in the view.

I don't give him long to look as I reach up and begin unbuttoning his shirt. He lets me get a few of the buttons undone before pulling the shirt off over his head in one easy movement, and now it is my turn to take in the view. Javier is as chiseled and perfect as I had imagined. He is lean and strong and I find myself fumbling with his belt and pants when his hands reach down to steady mine.

"Allow me," he says, as he takes off his pants and kicks them aside.

His erection is now barely contained by the David Beckham boxer-briefs he is wearing, and I am very eager to have him in my mouth. I start to drop to my knees, but Javier stops me.

"*Lo siento*," he says, which I remember means "sorry" in Spanish. "But I've been dying to taste you all evening."

"That's really not something you need to apologize for," I say with a laugh.

And now it is Javier on his knees, slowly sliding my panties down my legs and burying his face between my thighs. He picks me up and lays me back on the bed and appraises me with a look from head to toe.

"Almost forgot this." He reaches behind my back to unhook my bra and pulls it off me. He gives me that dimpled smile of his as he leans down to give me a kiss, then moves quickly to my breasts, which he has gathered as best he can in his hands, pressing them together. He plants open-mouthed kisses on them both, going back and forth, before pulling my left breast into his mouth as far as it will go and sucking on it, hard. He winds his tongue around my nipple and playfully nibbles at it. I thrust my pelvis almost automatically, and his hands leave to move southward.

As he continues his oral exploration of my chest, he brings his left hand under my ass and his right hand in between my legs to find me wet and waiting. He moans softly as his fingers playfully explore the area, then it's my turn to moan as he puts one of his fingers inside me. I arch my back, and he abandons my tits just long enough to kiss my exposed neck.

He pulls his finger out of me and licks it, keeping eye contact with me the whole time.

"Oh, *sí*," he says. "I knew you'd be delicious."

Before I have time to react to his statement, he has pulled my legs apart and begins kissing my inner thighs. The feeling is so amazing, but he is teasing me again. I move my body, trying to position myself so I can feel his mouth and tongue at my clit and beyond, and Javier laughs.

"Well, if you can't be patient, I suppose I can give you what you want."

And oh, does he. With both hands underneath my ass so I am raised to the position he wants me, Javier plunges his tongue inside me and begins thrusting in and out of me. His tongue is long and strong, as I hope another body part will be, and just when I think it can't feel any better, he brings his tongue out and uses it to find my clitoris. With strong, quick strokes, he tickles and licks me while bringing two fingers inside me to make the sensation even stronger. I convulse and come for him as he gives a satisfied moan of appreciation at my new wetness.

Javier makes his way back up my body, kissing every part of me as he gently lifts me fully onto the bed. He lies next to me and I realize he is still wearing his damn boxers. I start to pull them off. "My turn to taste you?"

"Oh no, no," he says. "My turn to fuck you."

"So, I don't have to do any of the work tonight? That hardly seems fair." I lean over to my nightstand to grab a condom.

"I wouldn't say that." He opens the condom and places it onto his long, straight, and damn near perfect dick. He nods toward himself, inviting me to straddle him, and I happily oblige.

As I lower myself onto him, we lock eyes and both smile. I ease myself up and down on him. He helps by holding onto my hips, keeping things slower than I probably would, but his pace is just right. I bounce in ecstasy for a few minutes, and soon I'm covered in sweat.

Javier sits up and brings his face in between my slick breasts, breathing me in and holding me tight as he sits inside me. From here, he lays me back so my head is at the foot of the bed, pulling my right leg up to his shoulder as he takes over and begins fucking me into oblivion. I'm unaware of just how long we go on like that, but I orgasm two more times, the second as he finally finds his finishing point and collapses beside me.

He pulls me into an embrace, and we are a sweaty, sticky mess, but I don't care. He kisses me tenderly before getting up to clean himself up. I assume he is coming back to bed, so when I see him getting dressed, I eye him quizzically.

"If I stay, I'm afraid I would make love to you all night," he says, answering my gaze.

"Again, not something that requires an apology," I laugh.

"Ah, but if we do everything together in our first night, will you not be bored with me in a week?"

"I highly doubt that."

"Perhaps," he says with a laugh. "But tonight has been perfect and I want to take you out again tomorrow night. I need my strength."

He leans down to kiss me goodbye and I try unsuccessfully to pull him back into bed.

"Patience," he says, before giving my naked ass a playful slap. "You need your rest, too. Trust me."

And with that, he's gone, and I fall into a blissful sleep. And since Javier told me to get my rest, I decide to take another nap before our date tonight.

Chapter Nine

January 3

I'm taking some time off from daydreaming about Javier to work on the perfect flavor to surprise him with on our date this week. Javier spends his Sundays with his family, so I unfortunately can't see him again until later this week, but we made last night count for a few days apart, so I suppose it's okay.

*

After playing soccer for about two hours, we decide we have worked up a sweat for long enough and Coach Javier says it's time to hit the showers. Like any good student, I happily follow orders. I barely have time to look around Javier's house before we're stripping our clothes off on our way to his bathroom.

I contemplate giving Javier a blow job in the shower, but that reminds me of Carter and I know I need to distract myself before thinking of him in this moment. Instead, as we step into his shower, I turn away from Javier and back myself into him, finding he's already raring to go.

"No point in getting clean before getting dirty again," I say as Javier enters me from behind, apparently completely in agreement with my assessment of the situation. We fuck quickly and hard, still in exercise mode from earlier in the night, then clean ourselves up in the shower.

As I step out, Javier hands me a towel and asks if I want to borrow something of his to wear while we cook and eat. I look down at my pile of sweaty clothes and figure this is probably a good idea. He leads me to the kitchen, with both of us wearing nothing but towels. He reaches into a drawer and pulls out two aprons and offers me one. I laugh but decide to wear it and nothing else as we gear up for what I can only assume will be one sexy meal. He ties his apron on, covering his cock, but leaving his perfect ass in full view. I tie mine on, leaving myself looking like a topless dancer with a really weird choice of costume.

"Well, I'll never be able to look at that apron again without getting hard," he laughs and pulls me to him for a kiss. He reaches down and grabs my bare ass as my breasts smoosh up against his hard chest, then he abruptly pulls away. "Dinner. Must make dinner."

"Pretty sure we'll need some calories to burn off later tonight," I say in agreement.

"Oh, hell yes we will."

I watch in amazement as he throws together a delicious dinner without using any sort of recipe to guide him. He offers me tastes as we go, asking my opinion on whether he should use more of this or that. He lets me take over for a bit as he goes to grab another ingredient and I give a little scream as a bit of the sauce splatters from the stove and hits me in the belly.

"Oh, poor baby," he says, running back to me and licking the sauce off me. "Better?"

"While you're down there…" I tease.

From his knees, Javier turns the dials on the stove so everything goes to simmer. I step away from the burners until I bump into the island in the middle of the kitchen. Javier follows on his knees and lifts my apron over his head when he gets to me. I open my legs for him and hear him mumble something in Spanish before he begins licking me all over.

"What was that?" I ask.

"I was joking that this is my new favorite appetizer," he says, taking a pause from his work. He brings me to quick climax and pops his head up from under my apron to look up at me and smile.

He stands and I look down to see his apron sticking up from his perfect erection underneath. As much as I'd like for him to fuck me on the counter, I decide to show him how talented my tongue is as well and drop to my knees. I untie his apron and let it fall to the floor as I take him into my mouth. He is longer than I am used to, so I bring my hands up to help me give attention to his entire shaft. I take special care to use all my favorite tricks, and Javier's moans confirm he is enjoying what I can do. I pull him out of my mouth just in time for him to come, and he looks down at me, slightly disappointed.

"You're not thirsty?" he asks.

"Uh, er, that's not my favorite appetizer," I say.

"Ah. If you'd ever like to try it, I hear I taste sweeter than most men."

"Oh, well, maybe," I stammer. "Hey, is dinner ready?" I quickly change the subject.

We each throw on a pair of boxers and one of Javier's T-shirts and sit down to dinner. My hair is air-drying and I have no makeup on at all, but I feel beautiful under Javier's gaze. It's amazing how quickly I feel at ease with him. We eat and drink wine, laughing about our unorthodox cooking methods.

When the meal is over, I clear our plates and take them to the sink.

"Leave them," Javier says, coming up behind me. "I have something better in mind."

His "something better" involves scooping me up and carrying me to his bedroom, and what comes next is most certainly more fun than doing the dishes. We start slowly, kissing and entwining our bodies together as our desire builds. I wonder to myself if we are going slow so Javier can take his time getting his third erection of the evening, but as he rolls me over onto my back and lies on top of me, I realize this is not the problem.

"Fuck me," I murmur in between kisses, reaching down to pull his T-shirt off me. He lets me pull the shirt off, but presses one finger to my lips, reminding me that taking it slowly builds the anticipation. I relax my body and resign myself to waiting, which I remember means he will give my body lots of attention in the meantime.

He reaches down to pull his own shirt off and presses back down on top of me so our chests are completely touching, while still keeping his weight on his arms so as not to crush me. We are both still wearing underwear, but I wrap my legs around him anyway and feel his hardness. He pulls away and inches down my body until his face is even with my breasts.

If I thought he took his time in this area last night, I realize that was nothing compared to tonight. I am licked, bit, sucked, and massaged until I feel numb and tingly there and completely wet between my legs. I assume from here that Javier will go down on me, but in quick movements, he has pulled off both pairs of underwear and thrusts into me, surprising me.

He looks me right in the eye as he comes in and out of me and the intimacy of the moment brings a tear to my eye. He kisses me and continues fucking me, keeping the rhythm varied from slow to faster until we both come again.

We fall asleep still connected and when I wake up around midnight, I smile to see his face next to mine. I reach out to touch the dimple in his cheek and accidentally wake him up.

"Sorry," I whisper. "Go back to sleep."

"Not so fast," he says, and we begin again where we left off, with me marveling that he's still up for another round, literally.

And so, as I work in the back area of one of my Sinfully Good locations, I know the perfect flavor to create. I know the early days with any man are bound to be full of these new, amazing feelings, but I feel something more than lust for Javier. I know I want him and can't get enough, and I know this feeling by only one word. And so, I take a bite of January's Flavor of the Month and smile. "Passionfruit-aholic" is truly delicious.

Chapter Ten

www.flavorsofthemonth.bloggerific.com

Well, we're through week one out of fifty-two for the year and I think this little experiment of mine is working out just fine so far. J and I spent most of the week apart, but we were able to catch up on Wednesday for lunch and I got to see him at work. He's great at his job and I can tell he really enjoys it!

We're going on date number three tonight and I'm hoping we can get to know each other even better. J's flavor is now officially available at all Sinfully Good locations. Mention this blog and get it for free this weekend. Pretty sure I still only have three people reading this, so enjoy the free ice cream, friends!

JANUARY 8

This might be the best first week of any year in the history of years. Okay, that might be overstating things, but really, I don't think so. Javier is busy getting his classroom in order and starting school again, which gave me time to get a few things done at work too. The beginning of the year is a busy time as I work through tax documents and annual budget reviews, but this year is even busier as I am putting together plans to hand over the day-to-day operations to my second-in-command, Samantha. Sam started out as a scooper at my first store when she was in high school, worked at the same store while she attended ASU, and I made her the manager of that store and two others when she graduated. She's sweet and smart and knows the Sinfully Good stores almost as well as I do. If I'm going to make this whole Plan thing a reality, I need to focus on that and step back.

Sam, who has been saying for years that I need to settle down with someone, could not be happier, and not just because I've promoted her to vice president of my company.

"Cyn! You're finally doing it!" she exclaims as we chat at a table at The Garden, our favorite lunch spot in Scottsdale. I've filled her in on the Plan and my first week with Javier, and she is so giddy she almost knocks her water off the table.

"I mean, I thought you and Carter would end up together, but this Javier guy sounds pretty amazing," she says. "Are you sure you want to keep going with the rest of the months? Why not give Javier a real shot and then just decide between the two of them?"

"Trust me, it's crossed my mind," I sigh. "But that's not what I told Javier when we started this and I'm really trying to follow through on what originally felt like a great idea."

"Well, if you're sure, I want to help. Why don't I share your blog on my social media pages and see if I can help you find someone for March?"

"That would be great."

I send her the link and tell her she's free to share it whenever, as I assume it will take a while to find someone who is on board with the idea. That's also probably a good thing, just in case Javier talks me into abandoning the Plan, which he easily could right now.

We aren't able to meet up for a proper date this week, but I do stop by the school on Wednesday to say hello and bring him lunch and a sample of his new flavor. We sit in his classroom eating and chatting for a few minutes before I casually mention I've always wanted to do it on a teacher's desk.

"Oh really?" Javier's eyes light up.

"Well, I mean, it's a pretty hot fantasy." I blushed. "In fact, I kinda dressed for the occasion in case you were up for it."

"Oh Cyn," he sighs, "I'm always up for you."

I open my trench coat to reveal the adult schoolgirl uniform and knee-high stockings I threw on before leaving the house, in anticipation of this very moment.

"Any chance I can earn some extra credit?" I say, as Javier runs to lock the door on his classroom and pull down the shade.

"I only have ten minutes before my next class," he says. "But I'm pretty sure I have time for a quick pop quiz."

He hurries back over to me, and I sit back on his desk, giving him a glimpse up my skirt where he sees I'm not wearing underwear.

"Now Ms. Blake," he says. "I do believe you are breaking the school dress code by not wearing panties. I'm afraid you'll have to stay after class for detention."

"Oh dear," I say, fully going along with the fun. "Will I be punished?"

I jump off the desk, turn around, and lift my skirt up, pointing my naked ass up at Javier. He gives me a light spanking, just as I hoped he would.

"Oh, you'll be punished." He spanks me again. I turn back around and face him, giving him my best "I've been naughty" face, and he laughs as he pulls down his pants.

"Seriously, Cyn, I don't have much time, so I'm going to fuck you fast, but please oh please wear this same outfit on our date this weekend."

"Yes, sir," I say as Javier begins fucking me as I sit on his desk. We go hard and make an absolute mess of the papers on his desk, but it's so damn sexy I don't think either of us cares. I reach over to where I've set his ice cream and find it a bit melted. I pour a little in between my tits and throw my head back as Javier licks it out then climaxes inside me. I hop off him and we assess the damage to his desk as we get dressed.

"Well, it looks like I'll need to go make more copies of this week's homework, as this stack is now covered in something I'm pretty sure would get me fired." Javier laughs, throwing a stack of papers into the trash can.

I laugh, too, thinking back on the memory of that day as I leave lunch with Sam and decide to stop by a Fascinations store for a few more dress-up items for tonight's date. If he enjoyed schoolgirl Cyn, I have a feeling we can have even more fun with what I've got in mind.

Chapter Eleven

www.flavorsofthemonth.bloggerific.com

Date number three was a tremendous success! I found a series of questions for J and I to ask so we could learn even more about each other. Here are some of the questions (and a few of our answers) in case you'd like to try them out on a date sometime soon:

1. Given the choice of anyone in the world, who would you want as a dinner guest? (I said Paul McCartney, J said me. Well, that's what he said at first, which made me blush, but then he changed his answer to his abuelita, who is back home in Spain and unable to travel. He misses her terribly and doesn't get to see her often. Awww.)

2. Would you like to be famous? In what way? (I said a pretty quick no to this, and J agreed, unless he was famous for making the world a better place, but not hassled by people in public. That's always been my main feeling as well. Paparazzi and everything else associated with the celebrity lifestyle has always made me feel nauseated.)

3. Before making a telephone call, do you ever rehearse what you are going to say? Why? (J said no and seemed confused by the question. Why wouldn't you just say what's in your heart or the first thing that comes to mind? Ah, he clearly has never been on the receiving end of one of my awkward phone calls where I'm not sure what to say. Yes, I rehearse. A lot. And not just for phone calls.)

4. What would constitute a "perfect" day for you? (J just smiled here and told me to wait until next Saturday so he could show me. Wahoo!)

5. When did you last sing to yourself? To someone else? (I told J I sing to myself all the time, but it's been years since I have sung for anyone else. He asked me to sing for him and I was too shy, but perhaps another day. He said he'll return the favor when I do. Perhaps part of our perfect day?)

6. If you were able to live to the age of ninety and retain either the mind or body of a thirty-year-old for the last sixty years of your life, which would you want? (Here, we were split, with me saying body and J saying mind. We've both watched relatives succumb to the perils of aging in different ways and moved on from this one pretty quickly before we got too bummed out.)

7. Do you have a secret hunch about how you will die? (Again, kind of a bummer, but J said he's always had a feeling he'll die young but uses that feeling to live each day to the fullest. I like the sentiment, but I moved on quickly, because again, bummer.)

8. Name three things you and your partner appear to have in common. (We both thought about this and wrote down our answers to compare. J wrote love of family/friends, health, and humor. I wrote kindness, surrounded by love, and fitness. Pretty close!)

9. For what in your life do you feel most grateful? (Here we were completely in sync—our families, both blood and friends.)

10. If you could change anything about the way you were raised, what would it be? (J clearly idolizes his parents and gave a quick answer saying he would change nothing. I can almost say the same, so I went with that as well.)

11. Take four minutes and tell your partner your life story in as much detail as possible. (We felt like we'd already done this one on our first date but went back through each other's pasts to see if we'd missed any crucial details.)

12. If you could wake up tomorrow having gained any one quality or ability, what would it be? (I said I'd want the ability to love without holding back because I'm always so afraid. J kissed me and said he'd want the ability to show me how to do that. Goooooood one.)

This is all from a series of thirty-six questions I found in the NY Times in an article about whether or not this series of questions could help strangers fall in love. I decided to only do the first third for now. Not sure about love, but boy oh boy do I think J is amazeballs!

JANUARY 9

Javier might just be the perfect guy. I'm starting to worry that we were focusing on our physical compatibility only, so I tell him sex will have to wait until he answers a few questions for me. And by a few, I mean twelve. He doesn't hesitate at all. In fact, he seems to enjoy the inquisition and likes asking me the questions too.

Where he easily could have given me silly or quick answers, he instead takes his time and gives me thoughtful, complete responses that help me fall even more for him. And since he gave me the courtesy of being such a good sport, I decide to reward him with a super fun evening with a bit of a reverse on the role-playing we did earlier in the week.

I excuse myself after our question-and-answer session and change into the outfit I put together before calling Javier back into my bedroom. I know he asked me to be the schoolgirl again, but I thought we might stick with the school theme with a twist. I've still got on stockings (thigh-high, this time) because he loves them, but I've thrown on a black pencil skirt and tight-fitting button-up dress shirt. The top buttons are undone, showing off a ridiculous amount of cleavage thanks to the get-up I have on underneath. I pull my hair back into a bun and secure it with a pencil, then throw on some fake glasses to complete my naughty librarian look. I grab the ruler I set aside and wait for Javier to arrive.

He comes into my room with wide eyes and a devilish smile.

"Are you my teacher now?" he says with a laugh.

"Actually, I'm your librarian and I'm afraid we have ourselves a bit of a problem. Sit down, Javier." I motion to the chair I've set up in the middle of the room.

Javier happily obliges, most likely because in his seated position he is now eye level with my breasts. I step closer and smile as he breathes in and reaches for me, but back up before he can touch me.

"No, no, no, Javier," I say. "I'm afraid you've been a bad boy and bad boys don't get to touch just yet. You've got to earn it."

"*Dios mio,*" he says. "Just tell me what to do."

I laugh, realizing I haven't really thought this through all that much, and now he's here I just want him to touch me. I thought I could be the one to drive him wild by calling for patience, but I honestly have no idea how he does it. I scramble for an idea to stall for time.

"Ummm…what's one plus one?" I say.

"*Dos,*" replies Javier.

"Correct!" I say, pulling the pencil from my hair. "Who was the first President of the United States?"

"George Fucking Washington," Javier says, starting to unbutton his shirt.

"I'm sorry, that's not quite correct, and I don't believe I said you could start undressing just yet. Turn around," I command.

Javier stands and turns and doesn't resist when I bend him over so his hands are on the chair. I give his ass a quick rap with the ruler.

"Now I kinda want to answer all of them wrong," he laughs as he sits back down.

"Oooh, so you like being punished, do you? Too bad, because I was just about to take the rest of this off," I tease, throwing my glasses aside, but leaving everything else on.

"No, no, ask me another. I'll be good," he begs.

"Okay, Javier. What letter comes after E?"

"F. As in fuck."

"Exactly."

I unzip my skirt and slowly slink it down my body as Javier pulls his shirt off. I let him stand to take off his pants, then walk around behind him to give his bottom a few more slaps with my ruler.

"I didn't say you could undress yet, but since you've already started, keep going," I say. "Then sit back down."

Javier removes his briefs and sits back on the chair, naked, erect and looking about as eager as I've seen him. I take off my blouse and let Javier take in the sight of me in the full ensemble: black push-up bra, black lacy crotchless panties that connect down to garter belts holding up my stockings. I know I look good and I figure we've waited long enough. I sit down on Javier's lap, not bothering to take anything off. I bring him inside me and kiss him, hard, on the mouth.

Javier grabs my ass with both of his hands to bring me up and down on top of him, first quickly, then he slows it down so he can take time to bury his face and mouth in my breasts as they come up to his level. I am in full tingly-below-the-waist mode now and clench and orgasm around him as his thrusts bring me to climax. The chair is a slippery mess and Javier picks me up to carry me to the bed, still inside me.

When we get to the bed, Javier pulls out for a moment and again picks me up.

"I'm going to take you from behind now, my naughty librarian," he says, turning me over so my top half is on the bed with my ass exposed at just the right level.

Standing behind me, Javier continues fucking me with one hand on my ass and the other coming underneath to grab my right breast. The hand on my ass leaves for a moment and comes back down with a light spank and I shudder.

"Where'd that ruler go?" he whispers.

"Nope, that's just for me to use," I laugh.

He sighs and gives me another open-handed spank. It's just the right level of pleasure and the quick sting of pain, plus the comfort of knowing Javier would never hurt me. He's using his spanking hand to rub my clit now and I find myself climaxing again, but we keep going. I am marveling at his stamina when I feel him give a few more thrusts before finishing.

We clean ourselves up and fall asleep naked, but when I wake up, he's gone. I am confused for a minute, but then I remember him saying he plays in a Saturday morning soccer league, so that must be where he is. I grab my computer to quickly get out today's blog post then get dressed to head to the gym. If he's working out, I suppose I probably should too. Besides, we've got another date planned for tonight and I can't expect to burn all my calories having sex, can I?

Damn, that would be nice.

*

It's been one of those Saturdays where I've had the perfect mix of productivity and chill. After working out, I come back and start some laundry and clean up a bit. I decide to reward myself by watching some *Downton Abbey* and snacking on popcorn, which is exactly what I'm doing when I receive a weird text from Sam.

Sam: *We're running out of this month's flavor at three of the stores. Did you leave the recipe list so I can make some more?*

Me: *How are we running out already?*

Sam: *That was my other question—how long am I supposed to be running the free ice cream promotion?*

Free ice cream? Why is she giving it out for free? The only people who should know about that are the readers of my blog, and don't I still only have friends subscribed? Unless…

Me: *Did you share my blog already?*

Sam: *Yes, actually! It got a bunch of shares. But those were just my friends. People are requesting free scoops all over the Valley.*

Okay, this is weird. I grab my laptop to open it when my phone rings. It's a local number I don't recognize, so I let it go to voice mail. I get to my blog and see it still says I only have three subscribers. I hit refresh just to make sure and my jaw drops just as my phone dings, indicating that I have a new voice mail.

I have 9,754 subscribers.

> **Me:** *SAM. How do I have almost 10,000 subscribers on my blog?? How many people liked it on your pages?*

> **Sam:** *Nowhere near that! But Channel 12 News just called here asking for you. Cyn...my friends in the media might have picked this up.*

Oh shit. Sam and I both have plenty of friends who work for local news outlets. But who could be interested in this blog? With a weird feeling in the pit of my stomach, I check my voice mail.

"Hi, Ms. Blake, this is John Sommers from Channel 12 News. We'd like to do a profile on your blog and maybe a recurring piece on how the search is going. Give me a call when you get this at 602-555..."

I don't even hear the last few numbers of his phone number because I am now doing a Google search for my name to see if this has been picked up online yet. The results almost make me spill my popcorn bowl everywhere. Almost. Under the watchful eye of Lady Grantham and family on *Downton Abbey*, I miraculously don't commit this faux pas. In fact, probably best to pause the show before I lose my shit.

> *Local Ice Cream Madam Searches for Mr. Right.*

> *Sinfully Single No More? You won't believe what Cynthia Blake is up to this year.*

> *Want to Play Matchmaker? Send your eligible bachelors to*

THIS site for a chance at…

Wait, what? They're already telling people to contact me about dates? I distantly remember setting up a Contact Me widget on the blog. I click on my email to see if anyone has responded and can't believe what I see: I have thirty-seven new messages, which appear to be from guys who'd like to date me or friends/family of potential guys who apparently do want to play matchmaker.

My phone dings again, this time with a new text. I assume it's Sam, so I ignore it for a minute as I read through some of the messages. Two of them have already started with "I don't normally do this, but…" Wow. Guess I'll have an easier time finding men for this little experiment than I thought. But wait—if I've gone *this* viral in a day, I am suddenly very nervous that this could explode. My phone dings again, pulling me from my minor freak-out.

Carter: *Um, did I just see you on Buzzfeed?*

Carter: *Cyn, what is going on?*

Buzzfeed? I thought this was just local? I take another look at the articles on my Google search, but I don't see that one. He must be confused. I go to Buzzfeed.com and look around, though, and sure enough, there is an article about me, but they've spelled my name wrong. For some reason, they've got it as Synthia Blake. I'm annoyed, but if it slows down the attention to my personal pages for a bit, that's fine with me.

I quickly log into my Facebook, Instagram, and all social media pages to make sure I've got my privacy settings on lockdown. They're loaded with friend requests and messages, but all seems to be in order in the privacy department. Thank God I've only referred to Javier as J on my site! He's a teacher and I'm pretty sure being associated with something like this might cause him issues. I grab my phone to text him when I realize I haven't responded to Carter.

> **Me:** *Sam shared my blog and local media picked it up and apparently I'm the new viral sensation of the year. Who knew??*

> **Carter:** *You mean who knew that men would be throwing themselves at you? *raises hand**

> **Me:** **blushes* Sweet, but not sure I wanted this much attention.*

> **Carter:** *Yeah, let me know if you want to shut the whole thing down. I'm not sure I want you to have this much attention either. Say the word and it's you and me.*

Wait, *what*? Didn't I offer that just last week? Wasn't I in full-on wedding planning mode when Carter told me to move forward?

Must stop and think.

On the one hand, I have Carter now scared back into wanting me. Carter, who knows and loves me and could be everything I've ever wanted.

On the other hand, in one week, I've found another seriously strong contender in Javier. I know that could very easily be infatuation, but it *feels* like more than that.

I'm about to resort to eenie meanie miney mo when my phone dings again.

> ***Javier:*** *Have seen your blog shared on Facebook about ten times now. Don't go jumping to all those new guys until I've had a chance to finish my month, okay?*

I need a drink.

Chapter Twelve

www.flavorsofthemonth.bloggerific.com

WELCOME TO ALL MY NEW READERS! Sorry for the caps, but there are so many of you that I want to make sure even people standing in the back can hear me. What? That's not how the internet works? Sorry, sorry—my bad. A little nervous with all the new attention here.

Anyway, I am still a bit in shock by how many of you have subscribed to this page. For those of you who have sent me notes asking to be one of my Flavors, I want to say THANK YOU (sorry—yelling again) and I am diligently reading through your notes. I already have a gentleman lined up for February and another for June, but there are nine spots available and I really can't wait to meet you guys.

J and I had a lovely date last night and we are both trying to wrap our heads around all of this attention. His flavor, Passionfruit-aholic, is still free at all Sinfully Good locations through the rest of the weekend, so if you want to give it, or any of our other delicious flavors a try, stop on by!

JANUARY 13

The last few days have been…weird. That's an understatement, but I'm honestly not sure what other word to use. Javier and I had a date Saturday night, but we opted to not have sex. He said he just wanted to slow things down and get to know me better, but I think he's just as weirded out about this whole "blog going viral" thing as I am. The date was still great (dinner and a movie, classic), but the air between us has changed.

Javier seems equal parts determined to win me over in this month and conflicted about whether I am actually worth it. He, like Carter, has really started to think about what it will mean for me to continue with the Plan for the rest of the year. Hell, even I am wondering what this will mean for me, both personally and professionally. I've been compared to *The Bachelorette* on countless blogs and news sites this week. And didn't only, like, one of those relationships work out? Granted, I'm giving each guy a month, away from cameras, and we don't have producers trying to force us into dramatic situations, but the parallels are real and scary.

And then there's Carter. Oh, my sweet Doctor of Hotness (a fun pet name we came up with a few years ago). Since Javier spends Sundays with his family, I asked Carter to come over so we could chat. He only had a short break from his schoolwork, but in those thirty minutes, I apparently showed enough confusion in my decision-making process that he made the decision for me (once again) to just continue with the Plan. Perhaps if I could have just looked him in the eye and told him I love him (which I have still yet to do), this whole thing could be over. But I didn't, and until I can do that earnestly without another man popping into my head, onward we go.

Speaking of onward, Javier has requested I set aside this weekend because he wants to show me what his perfect day looks like.

"You need a whole weekend to show me a day? Do days last longer in Spain?" I laughed as we chatted last night.

"Actually, yes, they do," he said, also laughing. "But only because we make them count more."

I sighed, dreaming of visiting Spain like I've always wanted to.

"But really," he continued, "Saturday is for the perfect day. Friday is to get to the perfect location and Sunday is to recover."

I am officially ready for Friday to hurry the hell up and get here.

Chapter Thirteen

January 17

It turns out that Javier's perfect day is just like Mary Poppins—practically perfect in every way. That might be the least appropriate time to reference Julie Andrews, especially considering certain parts of the perfect day, but whatevs.

When school gets out on Friday, Javier picks me up at my place. I've packed a weekend bag with the items he requested (casual clothes, sandals, one nicer ensemble for a dinner out, no makeup) so I'm ready to go, but puzzled by the disappointed look on his face when he sees me.

"I said no makeup," he says in a pretend pout.

"I didn't pack any. Want me to wash this off?"

"*Por favor*. I just want to see *you* this weekend."

I run back inside to remove any evidence that I tried to alter my appearance for him. Honestly, I don't wear much makeup to begin with and I'm comfortable without it. I guess it's just a habit to throw on a bit of mascara and such before I head out the door. But hey, I'm not going to complain about a man who likes me, just as I am.

My stomach does a little flip at the Mark Darcy-ness of the request. Javier most certainly isn't British or aloof, but could he be just what I'm looking for anyway?

We hit the road and drive west, so far that soon we are out of the Valley and on the familiar road leading to San Diego. I look over to Javier and raise an eyebrow.

"Just where are you taking me?" I ask.

"Well, I have the basics down, but you'll have to fill me in on the end of the directions," he says. "I thought we'd check out your little beach place. I asked Kim and she said you usually keep one of the rooms open and unrented."

"I do!" I practically shout. "I mean, I do," I say, more calmly. It's been ages since I've made the time to get there and I'm borderline giddy at the thought of seeing the ocean. It's a long drive for such a short trip, but ten hours of getting to know Javier on the way there and back when we are unable to have sex seems like a great plan. Plus, I'm excited that he's not driving me out to the middle of the desert to murder me, which seemed unlikely but is always good to avoid.

"How does your perfect day involve a place you've never been?" I ask.

"That's part of it, actually," he says. "I love to explore new places, and I love to make a woman happy, to see her in her comfortable surroundings. I know this is a special place to you and I love being by the ocean. My perfect day is any day where I can do things that feel amazing to me and my partner."

I ease back into my seat and smile at this thought. Javier has put together a playlist of Spanish music, mostly instrumental, for our ride, and it's a great soundtrack for the drive. The five-hour journey flies by and soon I'm directing Javier into the tiny garage attached to my house.

We're both hungry and looking to stretch after the drive, so I take Javier in for a quick tour and to drop off our things.

"The place is really better in the daylight hours," I say, as we set our bags in my bedroom. "There's great light and you can see the ocean right out that window."

"It's perfect, and I can hear the waves," he says, breathing in the salty air.

I so want him to love this place as much as I do and I'm happy to see that he seems at ease in the small space. The house itself is good sized, but since I rent it out to families and groups most of the year, I just have a small studio to myself when I come out. The bedroom is separated from the main space by a curtain Carter and I put up on one of our trips because we were on such different schedules at that point and we kept waking each other up. The curtain reminds me of how many times Carter and I have existed on different planes. Perhaps that's why we've never made (and maybe will never make) it work.

But for now, I'm face to face with Javier, who is here with me in this moment, completely. I grab his hand and we take a walk to one of my favorite little restaurants to grab some dinner. I love San Diego in the winter; the weather is temperate year-long, so it's not too cold, but the tourists are mostly gone, leaving the beaches and streets clear for residents and semi-residents, like me. We walk back to the house after dinner, still hand in hand, this time walking the quarter mile barefoot on the beach. I pull us to a stop on my spot, the area of sand directly in front of my house where I have spent countless hours basking in the sun, cuddling under blankets on cloudy days, and even shivering on chilly evenings like I am right now. Javier pulls me into a warm embrace, and we let the stillness of the moment be interrupted only by the sound of the tide coming up to kiss our toes.

"Thank you," I say into this shoulder.

With a gentle hand, Javier tips my face up to his and kisses me deeply.

"No, thank you," he says.

"*De nada,*" I reply.

*

We make love that night with the windows open, matching the

rhythm of the waves with our movement, Javier coming in and out of me until our passion leaves us both spent. It's not until the sun rises the next morning that we both stir and look around.

"You were right," he says. "Everything here is more beautiful in the light."

He is looking right at me when he says it and my cheeks flame under his gaze. I move toward the end of the bed, leaving the covers behind me as I stand to stretch. I turn to see Javier eyeing my naked body lustfully and wonder if I'm about to be pulled back down when he rises and begins to dress.

"Don't worry," he says, seeing my face fall a bit. "I'll take care of you plenty of times today."

We both laugh and head out of the door in search of breakfast. I lead us to a familiar spot, the Firehouse American Eatery. It is familiar in name and location but has changed so much from when I used to come here with my family as a kid. But still, eating on the rooftop patio is enough to make me happy, and I have fun sharing old stories with Javier as we enjoy our omelets and mimosas.

On our way out of the door, Javier pauses on the stairs and I turn to look up at him.

"What is it?" I ask. "Did you forget your wallet?"

"You seem a bit sad with all of your memories here," he says thoughtfully.

"I'd say more nostalgic than sad. I just need to make more

memories in the new space, I suppose. This is a good start."

"Want an even better one?" He grins.

He passes me on the stairs and grabs my hand, pulling me into the bathroom marked "family" before I even realize what's going on.

"There was no one around," he says. "I saw an opening."

I laugh and think this over. Having sex in the bathroom here would certainly be a new memory, but with how long Javier tends to last, I'm sure we'll be caught. My rising desire and nervousness about breaking rules are at complete odds in my head.

Sensing this, Javier steps toward me and says, "I can be quick when I want to be, Cyn."

I nod. "You better be."

After gaining my permission, Javier works quickly, pulling my panties off and throwing them on top of his head, like a frat boy in a bad coming-of-age movie. I barely have time to laugh as he pulls my skirt up and presses me up against the wall. His dick is out and erect and I drop to my knees to work a little tongue magic, assuming this will help to speed things up.

He pulls me to a standing position again after about thirty seconds, whispers a quick "*gracias*," then we're off. Fucking against the wall in a public bathroom is a first for me, but with how comfortable Javier seems with the whole situation, I wonder if it isn't for him. I'm just getting ready to ask him when someone knocks on the door.

"Occupied!" yells Javier, shaking his head as he tries to focus again on what we're doing. I'm about to say we should abort this mission when Javier explodes inside me. I clean myself up as quickly as I can and grab my panties off his head, now blushing profusely at having to face whoever is waiting outside the bathroom.

"Give me twenty seconds, then come out," he says, ducking out of the door.

I have no idea what he can do in twenty seconds, but I do as I'm told, open the door a smidge, then run out, realizing the coast is somehow clear. I catch a glimpse of Javier talking to a mother and her young son with their backs turned toward me as I head for the exit and can't help but smile. If he's a smooth enough talker to convince me to both blow him and fuck him in a bathroom, I shouldn't be surprised he's charming a stranger to give me a clean exit.

"What did you say to her?" I ask, as he comes out after me, laughing to himself.

"I said I was helping my drunk friend use the bathroom and it would probably be best to give him a minute to clean up the place," he says, clearly pleased with himself and starting to crack up.

"How'd you get them to turn their backs?" I ask, impressed.

"I said it was too early for a kind woman and young child to see a grown man covered in his own vomit."

Okay, now I'm the one cracking up.

*

The rest of Javier's perfect day consists of snuggling on the beach with me, sharing headphones listening to another playlist he's put together, napping on blankets in the sand, throwing a Frisbee back and forth by the water, walking down to Belmont Park to ride the roller coaster, and a full-on oral sex marathon back at the house after we've headed back for dinner.

Marathon is the only way to describe it for the sheer duration. I start by turning on Javier as soon as we walk in the door and dropping to my knees. It's weird, but I swear the salty air makes everything sexier, and I'm eager to have him in my mouth. We move to the bed where I continue going down on him until he finishes. I lay back next to him as he says, "That was nice, but now you rest."

I assume we're going to take a second nap (my perfect day involves two naps), but what comes next is, well, me. Multiple times.

Javier spends so much time between my legs that I figure he'll have to start getting his mail delivered to my pussy. He fingers me, licks me, and tongue fucks me until I'm numb and honestly not sure I can take anymore. I've lost count of my orgasms, mostly because I can barely think straight, but Javier says it was three that he's sure of, with maybe a few mini ones thrown in. I wait in anticipation of another delicious fucking when he says, "Time to get dressed for dinner."

I look at the clock and can't believe it's already after seven o'clock. I can't quite remember what time we got home, but I know Javier just spent a solid hour eating me out.

"How can you even still be hungry?" I quip.

He throws his head back to laugh and I catch the smile that makes me weak. I am feeling a bit hungry myself, so I get up to shower and get ready for dinner, offering to order in if Javier is also feeling like just staying in.

"I want to show you off tonight, *querida,*" he says.

Hard to say no to that.

*

We dress and take a cab to the Gaslamp district of San Diego for dinner at the US Grant hotel. It's posh and pretty and we are dressed to the nines. Javier looks completely *GQ* in his designer jeans and dress shirt, and I'm feeling pretty good in a little black dress that hugs me in all the right places. I'm wearing wedge heels I can walk comfortably in, but that bring my height up to five eleven and make my legs look impossibly long. Even sans makeup and with my hair in a simple braid, Javier insists I am turning heads as we walk downtown and into the restaurant.

I can almost feel eyes on me and wonder where this confidence has come from. I am borderline strutting, reflecting Javier's demeanor, perhaps. We head straight for the lounge area, having arrived about fifteen minutes before our reservation, and order from the Billionaire Cocktail list, drinks that are both top shelf and extremely potent. On an empty stomach, I find myself deliciously tipsy after one drink and ready for the decadent dinner that follows.

We order encore drinks with dinner and share one of my favorite desserts in the whole world (mango beignets), which reminds me of the Passionfruit-aholic flavor ice cream I've made for Javier. Everything feels unbelievably sexy, and I can't tell if it's the alcohol coursing through my system or the connection I feel to Javier.

Whichever it is, I find myself unable to keep my hands off him. We snuggle up close in our booth and I am fondling Javier through his pants before he scolds me and warns that we likely can't get away with a bathroom rendezvous twice in one day. I pull back and we leave the restaurant.

Once the night air hits me, I shiver a bit, and the goose bumps rise on my skin immediately. Javier throws his blazer over my shoulders as we wait for the Uber he's requested, but I turn around to kiss him while we wait, almost dropping his jacket to the ground. He picks it up and steadies me, and I can see in his eyes that this passion I'm feeling is most certainly on both sides of this equation.

Our Uber driver pulls up and Javier goes around to the driver's side door to ask a question in Spanish, assuming correctly that the driver also speaks the language. He comes back to open my door for me and says, "I told him I'd throw him a big tip if he keeps his eyes on the road. I can't keep my hands off you and know you don't like an audience."

I grin and slide across the backseat. There's not really enough room for full-on sex, so I'm not sure what Javier has in mind, but I figure I won't have to wait long to find out. Javier sits down next to me and I close my eyes, expecting him to keep kissing me, but instead feel his lips on my neck as his hands find the zipper on the back of my dress. He unzips it to the small of my back and slides the straps down, bringing my naked breasts into full view. I love this dress because it doesn't need a bra and I'm suddenly mentally high-fiving myself for the decision.

We spend the whole drive home with Javier's hands and mouth expertly taking care of my tits, one at a time and together, and the whole thing is so hot I am mentally envisioning fucking him right here and now when we pull up to my house. People may have seen us along the drive, but the driver kept his word (I think. Actually, who the fuck cares?) and Javier throws him some extra cash, as I pull my straps back up for the short walk into the house.

I drop my dress as soon as we are both inside and stand naked, waiting for Javier to come in. He walks directly to me and begins kissing me hard as his hands explore my back, ass, and in between my thighs, which has become a wet and warm spot, eagerly awaiting him.

"Mmm," he moans, feeling my wetness on his hands and bringing it up to lick his fingers.

"You are *seriously* overdressed," I say, starting to undo Javier's belt. I struggle with it as he removes his shirt and realize I might be tipsier than I realized. I love drunk sex, but I do tend to agree to crazier things in bed in this state than I normally would. I've never done anything I regret, but after our close call with my ass the other night, I make a mental note to watch my alcohol intake on future dates this year. Had this been the other night with Javier, I likely would have offered my ass up to him and said something about loving being fucked there, hard.

We're both naked now and making our way to the bed. Javier falls on top of me, and into me, in one movement. I cry out in sheer pleasure, my senses heightened by the intense foreplay and alcohol. We fuck missionary for a while until I indicate I want him to roll over onto his back. I turn myself around and back myself on him in a fun position I learned in college called reverse cowgirl. I find I have more control than traditional girl-on-top from here and it points Javier's dick right into my G spot.

It apparently feels good to Javier, too, as this is the position that brings him to climax. I bounce off him and lead him to the shower, where we take turns cleaning each other off before stumbling back to bed to pass out, naked, wet, and satisfied.

*

Javier wakes me up impossibly early in the morning (5:00 a.m.!) but says all I need to do is get dressed and climb in the front seat. I argue and say no, I'd be happy to keep him company on the drive home, but seeing as how I wake up as we pull up to my condo around eleven, I suppose that was an absolute lie. Javier walks me in to make hoping he's heading where I want him now. He drops to his knees, and I wrap my legs around his shoulders as he buries his face between my thighs. Instead of pulling my panties down and off, he gently moves them to the side with his fingers as he expertly locates my clitoris with one finger while putting another inside me.

I let out a loud moan of sheer pleasure as he flicks and rubs my clit while now bringing two fingers in and out of me at the same time. He pauses for a second to lick his fingers, gives out his own moan, and presses his mouth onto me. He's using his tongue on my clit now and moving it faster and harder than you'd think a tongue could move. It's so good and hot I feel like I might pass out.

"Fuck me," I breathe, knowing I'm going to come any second.

Patience be damned, I think to myself as he tears my panties apart in his strong hands. He's standing again in 1.5 seconds and thrusting into me before I have a moment to realize what's happening as I orgasm and shudder on his second thrust.

"That's one," he says. "Number two can happen when I'm ready, too, okay?"

I nod, unable to speak as I come down from the bliss. We're fucking hard now, and I tighten my legs around his body, trying to pull him into me more and more. He's happy to oblige and puts his hands firmly on my hips to match my rhythm and intensity. I feel like a rag doll in his strong hands, even more so when he quickly pulls out and flips me over in one move.

"Oh yes," he says, admiring the view. He puts himself back inside me and reaches around to cup my breasts as he takes me from behind. I know I can't last long in this position without coming again and reach down to help myself along.

"Ready to come again already?" he asks, moving a hand down to bat mine out of the way.

"Mmm hmmm," I say, feeling the tide rising inside me.

"Okay, okay, hang on." He moves his finger on my clit in a circular motion as his thrusts become harder and similarly paced. It takes about ten seconds until I can't hold on any longer, and I let out a moan that becomes a scream as I come and so does he. We curl up on the bed together, him still inside me, and both fall back asleep in a hot, sticky heap.

Chapter Twenty

www.flavorsofthemonth.bloggerific.com

I'm excited to announce that this month's flavor is called Sweet Surprise. I'm not telling you what's in it, but you're going to love it. I've met my fella this month; we'll call him K. He's really great, but not at all what I expected. I'm still checking my messages to find the rest of my suitors and can't thank you all enough for your submissions. I should really warn you all that I'm not nearly as amazing as you seem to think, but flattered nonetheless.

Enjoy this month's free flavor and don't forget about our speed dating event this Thursday!

Email submission from blog:

Dear Cynthia,

I'm a 33-year-old lawyer who lives in Scottsdale and I'd love to take you out sometime. I drive a luxury car, live in a million-dollar condo, and can give you the life you deserve. I know you're doing well with your ice cream shops, too, so you're not just going after guys with money. But this way we'll both know we like each other for more than what's in our bank accounts.

I have season tickets to the Diamondbacks I usually give out to clients, but since you're into it, we could definitely go to some games together. I think you're the total package and I'd love to get together for one of your months. I'm ready to settle down. Let's talk.

Joey

Ick. I honestly feel icky after reading that. Although, he does make a good point about the money thing. I hadn't considered the fact that some guys might just want to date me because I'm successful. I have literally no idea how to gauge that now. Thanks for totally freaking me out, Joey.

I send Peter Donovan an email.

Re: Mr. March submission

Dear Peter,

Of course I remember you! I was thrilled to hear from you and think you'd be a great Mr. March if you're still up for it. I love going to Spring Training games and I'm sure we'll have a great time. My schedule is wide open for your month, so feel free to make some plans and we'll chat again at the end of the month to set up a first date.

XOXO,

Cynthia

Chapter Twenty-One

February 4

Ken and I went on a proper date last night and I'm still kicking myself for judging him as just a fling before meeting him. Sure, he's sexy and we have great chemistry, but there's so much more to him than that. I loved the question exercise I did with Javier, so I figured I'd give it a go with Ken. Honestly, I was sorta hoping he would give some weird or terrible answers so I could un-confuse myself, but he did all right.

1. Given the choice of anyone in the world, who would you want as a dinner guest? (Ken said some famous race car driver whose name I can't remember. I may not remember who he said, but the why was really nice, even though I'm just not that into cars. He said the guy built

his car business from scratch and has always worked really hard to make a name for himself in the sport. Ken loves to work on cars, so I can totally see why he'd want to meet a hero in his field.)

2. Would you like to be famous? In what way? (Ken said he wouldn't mind being famous if he was known for an achievement and not something dumb. He hates reality TV and wouldn't ever want that kind of fame, but if he were successful and others took note, he'd be okay with that. I usually say no to this question, but I could see being okay with it under Ken's definition.)

3. Before making a telephone call, do you ever rehearse what you are going to say? Why? (Ken blushed and said yes to this one. He gets nervous calling everyone and said it took him about a day and a half to work up the nerve to call me. It was adorable.)

4. What would constitute a "perfect" day for you? (Ken loves going on road trips to places he's never been before, so a perfect day would probably consist of getting lost and stumbling upon something beautiful.)

5. When did you last sing to yourself? To someone else? (Ken seemed confused by this and does not appear to be musically inclined. Not a deal breaker by any means, but a bit of a downer.)

6. If you were able to live to the age of ninety and retain either the mind or body of a thirty-year-old for the last sixty years of your life, which would you want? (Ken said body here, then made a joke about sad people who let themselves go as they get older. At least, I hope he

was joking. It was kinda mean.)

7. Do you have a secret hunch about how you will die? (Ken said he hopes it's something instant like a car crash or a plane crash. Both of those are nightmares for me, so I pretty much just shuddered and moved on.)

8. Name three things you and your partner appear to have in common. (I said we're both fit, funny, and kind. Ken said that's the first time a girl he's dated has said he's funny. Did I make that up in my head? Is he not funny? Hmm.)

9. For what in your life do you feel most grateful? (Ken said he's thankful for his health, job, and freedom. I kinda get the feeling he's not super close with his family, but I guess I'll find out about that later.)

10. If you could change anything about the way you were raised, what would it be? (Ken said he'd probably make lots of changes, but he's happy with how he turned out, so maybe not. Again, I wonder what his family is like.)

11. Take four minutes and tell your partner your life story in as much detail as possible. (Ken gave me the basics, but trying to get details here was like pulling teeth. Come to think of it, he only spoke for about a minute. Time to play detective and see what else I can uncover.)

12. If you could wake up tomorrow having gained any one quality or ability, what would it be? (Ken said he'd want to be strong enough to lift a car over his head. I'm not really sure why, but hey, he works on cars, so maybe that would be super helpful?)

After the question-and-answer portion of the evening, Ken and I met a few of his friends at a bar for trivia night. I love trivia and so do his friends, so I assumed Ken would, too, but he derailed quickly after an unfortunate incident in the early rounds. As we crowded around the table at Carly's Bistro, a great little spot downtown, the woman running trivia announced the next category as Movie Quotes. Now, I know I'm a bit of an expert in this area, but I didn't want to seem too pushy with a group of people I don't know.

"Play it, Sam. Play 'As Time Goes By,'" said the trivia hostess.

"*Casablanca*!" I said in unison with a few of the guys at our table.

"Yeah, it's from *Casablanca*," said Ken, "but she said it wrong. The line is 'play it *again*, Sam.'"

"Actually, she got it right, but that's a pretty common misconception," I said.

"Uh, no, everyone knows it's 'play it again,'" said Ken. "I'll tell her when I turn in our answer sheet. She probably just said it wrong."

Now, I was 98 percent sure of myself, but I opted to leave it and went to get our group another round of drinks at the bar. The category ended, and I saw Ken walk up to the trivia lady with a truly obnoxious swagger. I saw him lean in for the mansplaining and was proud to see her shake her head and hold her ground. First of all, she was right, and second of all, even if she were wrong, we all knew which movie was the answer, so it really isn't something to make her feel bad about.

Ken stormed back to our table at the same time I came back with the drinks, but because he was staring at his phone, he didn't see me, and I dropped one of the drinks in the ensuing collision. He immediately snapped out of his quest to look up the quote, helped me clean everything up, and apologized profusely. We ended up coming in second place in the game and had a great rest of the evening.

*

As we walk into my place later that night, I have a weird urge to bring up the movie quote again. I have a terrible need to correct people from time to time, especially when they are being cocky the way Ken was with the really nice woman at the bar. I turn around after hanging my purse and keys inside the door to say something but am immediately distracted by Ken's urgency as he closes the distance between us and wraps me up in a strong kiss/embrace situation against the wall.

"You're amazing," he says in between kisses. "You're so smart and confident. I could barely keep my hands off you tonight."

Did he just insinuate that he finds my brain sexy? Oh, hell yes. If a guy likes me because I'm good at trivia, he's about to get super lucky.

We're still pressed up against each other and the wall, so I do a little jump into his arms and wrap my legs around his hips.

"Did you ever see *Jerry Maguire*?" I whisper playfully into his ear. "Cuz there's a scene I've always wanted to recreate."

I'm picturing Tom Cruise and Kelly Preston having crazy sex up against the wall. I can't wait to do my best impression of her when she yells, "Don't ever stop fucking me!" right here in my entryway. Ken seems to be on the same page as he pulls my shirt over my head, nodding and smiling.

"I love that movie," he says. "You're on."

We're both naked in about twenty seconds and he's inside me so fast I gasp. I'm about to throw my head back and deliver the line just like she does in the movie when Ken says, "Show me the money."

I tilt my head to the side and barely stifle a giggle as he repeats it, a little louder this time. "Show me the money, baby. Oh yeah, show me the money."

I realize where this is going and it is now taking every ounce of concentration I have not to crack up at this misunderstanding as Ken is clearly lost in his own fantasy, fucking me against a wall and shouting, *"Show me the money! Show me the money!"*

He finishes quickly, then gently carries me to my bed where he lays me down, cups my face in his hands, and says, "You had me at hello. You had me at hello."

It's so sweet. It really is and I'm trying to focus on the fact he thinks he's just given me great sex combined with a romantic finish for the ages. I do love that "had me at hello" line, although I think I'm the one who is supposed to say it. But now Ken is showering and I'm desperately trying to figure out what the hell just happened. *It's sweet,* I tell myself. *But it's weird,* says another voice in my head. Maybe it's the conundrum of those two schools of thought, or maybe it's because

I just had my head slammed against a wall one too many times, but I'm soon asleep and left to decipher the evening's events another day.

Chapter Twenty-Two

www.flavorsofthemonth.bloggerific.com

Thank you to everyone who came out to our speed dating event last week! It was a huge success and I definitely felt like I witnessed several love connections happening all around me. A few attendees asked me to go into a bit more detail about who I'm looking for with this whole thing, and I can only think of one way to explain it. I'm looking for my Jess. Or my Luke, if you prefer to focus on Lorelai. I am, of course, referring to Gilmore Girls, which is going to be required viewing for whoever I end up with (bonus points if you're already a fan!).

You see, there are three main suitors for Rory's affections over the course of the show: Dean, Jess, and Logan. Whoever you're rooting for of those three says a lot about who you're looking for in life. Dean is Rory's first boyfriend. He is stable, charming, handsome, but not nearly as smart as Rory. He has grown up with a mother who stays home and cooks every night and there is literally nothing wrong with that, but it shapes who he is and what he wants out of a relationship. Basically, he doesn't want Rory and he's not right for Rory, no matter how much he loves her.

In college, Rory meets Logan and immediately hates him. He is rich, good-looking, cocky, smart, and immature. And oh, is he charming. Eventually, Rory falls for him, but he brings out the worst in her. Rory has a tendency to go off course when met with resistance and Logan is more than happy to stand by as she flounders. Eventually, he makes the same mistake as Dean, thinking he can convince Rory to move across the country with him, abandoning her dreams and settling down well before she is ready.

And then there's Jess. Jess shows up while Rory and Dean are together and eventually causes enough havoc between them that Dean breaks up with Rory when it becomes clear she is already falling for Jess. Though the entire town and her mother hate Jess, Rory sees him like no one else can. He is smart, well-read, sarcastic, loyal, funny, and loves Rory too much to let her settle or doubt herself. When Rory drops out of Yale, Jess is the only one who can get through to her to get her back on the right path. He goes from sullen teenager to confident young man as the series progresses and eventually eclipses both Dean and Logan as the right choice for Rory.

His love for Rory, like Luke's love for Lorelai, is the kind of love I want. I want someone who sees who I am, flaws and all, and loves me anyway. I don't need someone to pretend I'm perfect, because I don't expect them to be. I need someone who will challenge me to be the best version of myself. So if you're a Dean or a Logan, or even a Max or a Christopher (seriously, watch the show if you don't already), no need to apply. But if you're the Luke to my Lorelai or the Jess to my Rory, I can't wait to meet you.

FEBRUARY 5

"Wait, wait—he did not scream out 'show me the money' while you guys were having sex. I refuse to believe that."

I wasn't planning to tell Meg about the Jerry Ma-fucking-guire incident, but apparently two glasses of wine are enough to get me to spill my secrets. I should never become a spy. I'd probably give away all of our nation's secrets halfway through a bottle of Pinot Noir.

"He did and it was the weirdest thing ever and now I'm legitimately not sure how to look him in the eye," I say. It's an overreaction, to be sure, but wine also makes me a bit dramatic.

"I mean, it's not the best, but I can't think of a dumber reason to rule a guy out than getting a movie quote wrong mid-coitus."

There it is—that's the perspective I need. I mentioned a movie and he immediately thought of the most famous line. That's not weird. If anything, he probably thinks I'm weird for wanting him to scream "show me the money" while we were fucking. He might be sitting at a table with a friend right now saying, "I have no idea why, but she must just really like that movie." Oh God, I hope that's not happening.

"Anyway," I say, hoping to steer the conversation anywhere but here, "how's the last-minute wedding-prep going? How can I help?"

"Oh, er, everything's fine," she says, suddenly finding the table fascinating.

"How can that be? Weren't you saying you still had favors and centerpieces to make? I thought we were doing marathon wedding sessions this weekend?"

Meg is now darting her eyes around the restaurant in a terrible attempt at avoiding eye contact with me when she finally sighs, shrugs, and comes clean.

"Kim and I finished most of that stuff this week. I am *not* getting in the middle of this, and I know you will respect that, but she offered to help and I didn't want to say no."

"In the middle of what?" I'm a bit gobsmacked.

"Whatever this thing is between you guys. I don't even know what all she's mad about and I frankly don't want to because then I'd have to choose sides, but she's pretty pissed, and you should probably call her. I don't need my bridesmaids glaring at each other behind my back in all the wedding photos. Please, just be the bigger person and see if you can fix this."

"I know she's pissed about something, but you know it will take her forever to tell me," I press. "Please, just give me a bit of a hint and I promise I'll be the bigger person. But I should probably know what I'm apologizing for before I actually see her."

"Well, I think she doesn't like how you treated Javier," says Meg slowly. "I'm not sure where it's coming from, but she kept saying she doesn't get how you could make him fall in love with you and then just move on."

"But—"

"I *know* it's part of the Plan." She cuts me off before I can protest. "But there's a difference between hearing about a plan and seeing it in action. She is friends with Javier. Maybe she just thought if you guys hit it off, you'd call things off and live happily ever after or whatever."

Okay, now I can't even be remotely annoyed with her. Haven't I been feeling the same guilt over what my Plan has done to other people? First it was Carter, then Javier, and now Kim. It doesn't matter that

I still think this could be the right path for me; if I'm causing this much hurt a little over a month in, how is this going to work for ten more months? I definitely like Ken, but I don't at all feel connected to him like I do Javier or Carter. I'm suddenly dizzy and agitated and now Meg is looking at me with real concern.

"She's right." I nod. "I'll call her, and we can talk it through. Don't worry. No angry bridesmaids will ruin your big day."

Chapter Twenty-Three

February 13

I really did mean it when I told Meg Kim and I wouldn't ruin her day. I meant it when I went home that night and sent Kim a text asking if we could meet for coffee the next day, and I definitely meant it walking into the shop to see her. I meant it all the way up to the moment when I went to give her a hug and was met with ice daggers being shot my direction from her normally kind eyes.

"I want you to know I'm sorry," I say, still a bit taken aback from her non-greeting.

"I believe you think that," she says, not budging an inch.

"I mean, I can't honestly see how any of this affects *you.*" I cross my arms, ready to dig in.

"Of course you can't," she spits back.

"We're a week from the wedding and you're clearly super pissed." I try to get us back on track. "Any chance we can put a pin in this for Meg and hash it out after the wedding?"

Kim softens a bit and I know I've taken the right approach.

"Yes," she says. "Of course. I don't really feel like talking about it right now anyway, so let's just tell her all is well and get through this next week."

*

We did a great job for honestly 99 percent of the wedding week. When family and friends started arriving, Kim and I cordially texted back and forth, helping to arrange rides, answer questions, pick up last-minute items and basically make sure Meg didn't get overwhelmed. I saw Ken a few times, but he was really understanding and said he'd been to enough weddings to know bridesmaids are crazy busy leading up to it. He did tell me to make sure to wear something super-hot under my bridesmaid dress on the actual day, though, because he'd always heard that nailing a bridesmaid is the best sex ever. I was already way ahead of him there but figured I could let him think it was his idea.

When the rehearsal rolled around, Kim, Meg, and I were the perfect bride/bridesmaid team, making sure everyone knew where they were supposed to be, keeping all conversations light and handing out last-minute directions to the dinner to be held later that night. To any outsiders, we were the three best friends anyone ever had.

And then the day of the wedding comes. This morning, we woke up in our hotel suite to a knock on the door to find that Fred and the boys had sent over breakfast and flowers for us with a special gift for the bride (diamond earrings, an excellent choice).

"Dear Meg, here's a little 'something new' for my beautiful bride. I'll see you soon. Love, Fred." Meg gets a bit choked up as she reads the card aloud to us.

"Aww!" I shriek. "What a sweetie. I'm so happy for you, Meg."

"Yeah, Meg," says Kim. "He's perfect. You guys are going to be so happy."

We all dry our eyes and nibble on the food before the hair and makeup team we'd booked arrive. I notice Kim taking a bit longer to compose herself but decide to sidestep that landmine and just focus on the day. She catches me looking at her and we immediately both avert our eyes, remembering our vow of keeping our damn mouths shut. It's a weird feeling to see her clearly upset, but not feel like I can help. However, seeing as how I'm the one upsetting her, I figure it best to just keep moving.

After a few hours of primping, we button Meg into her beautiful lace dress. She looks so stunning we all again have to blink back tears, but the tone has shifted, and I take the opportunity to attempt peace. I grab Meg and Kim's hands and says, "Meg, it is an honor to stand beside you today. Kim and I both love you so much."

"We do," says Kim. "But if you panic on the way down the aisle, we will drive you straight to the airport and whisk you to Mexico in a heartbeat."

We all burst into laughter and it's the perfect friend moment. Kim always knows how to defuse an emotional situation with laughter, especially when I'm the one bringing us all to tears with my sappy sentiments. I'm starting to feel like maybe all has been forgiven between us.

The wedding goes off without a hitch, and we manage to take group pictures in record time before hitting the cocktail hour then being announced at the reception. This is where I think things start to come off the rails.

You see, when you are a bridesmaid, you are running around like crazy the day of the wedding. Sure, we ate a bit in the morning, but eating after getting hair and makeup done is tricky, and by the time a glass of champagne is placed in your hand, it might be about five hours since you've had anything to eat or drink. Suffice it to say, Kim and I get tipsy. Fast.

I'd seen Ken when I walked down the aisle and beamed under his gaze. He looked gorgeous in his navy-blue suit, and I quickly flashed to what it might feel like walking down an aisle to him at the end of the year. It gave me a quick flutter, but as I took my place by the altar to see Kim walking toward me, I saw her also notice Ken, but in a very different way. Her gracious smile turned to consternation for a split second, imperceptible to anyone but me.

She hates Ken, I realized. *That's what this is all about.*

So sure am I about this realization I feel 100 percent empowered by champagne to mention it to Kim as we're getting ready to be introduced at the reception.

"Hey," I say, pulling her into a quick embrace. "You don't like Ken and that's fine. I totally get it and I'm sorry if you didn't want him here. I didn't get it, but I do now."

"Uh, no, you don't get it," she snaps, pulling away from my hug, then mumbling something under her breath that is quickly lost to the music blaring in the other room.

"What was that?" I hope to clear the air before we go in for dinner. I really did just mean for her to repeat herself to me, but neither of us could have anticipated the doors opening and the quiet hush that would fall over the assembled guests as she yells back what she had previously whispered.

"I just hate to see you being such a slut."

*

If you've never been a bridesmaid who was called a slut in front of the entire party by another bridesmaid, I'm not sure you can truly appreciate how awkward the rest of this night is. I try to play Kim's words off as a joke, as does she, once we both see everyone staring at us. To keep up appearances, we even hurl words like "Bitch! Slut! Skank!" at each other from across the dance floor all night. See. Everyone? Just a joke. A horribly inappropriate joke, but that's how we roll.

Except that's not at all how we roll, and Kim has broken one of the cardinal rules of our friendship: thou shalt not judge the promiscuity (or lack thereof) of another friend. We both throw ourselves back into full bridesmaid mode and light up the dance floor all night, but we've had a hand in semi-ruining Meg's special day and there will be hell to pay.

Ken looks taken aback by the whole situation but is a great date. Between getting me drinks and making sure I also eat my dinner and drink water, he helps me maintain a nice buzz throughout the evening without overdoing it. He asks me to dance at each slow song and by the end of the night, I am actually able to enjoy myself, and am certainly looking forward to the rest of the night as Ken holds me close.

"I hope you took my advice and wore something truly naughty under this dress," he whispers into my ear while the DJ plays "All My Life" by K-Ci and JoJo.

"Oh, I did," I whisper back. "Haven't you heard? I'm a slut."

He chuckles a bit into my hair. "I've never really been a fan of that word, but could maybe get on board with it, just for tonight."

I laugh, take his hand, and walk us off the dance floor. Meg and Fred have already done the whole grand exit thing, so I feel comfortable in abandoning the rest of the party in favor of getting my gorgeous date to our hotel room.

A few minutes later, we stumble into the elevator on the way up to the suite I've booked us for the night. Ken is quickly all over me, kissing my neck furiously as we ascend. We barely hear the doors open but manage to get out just before they close again, and I drag him down the hall to our room.

Once inside the door, Ken sits on the bed and looks at me intensely. All he says is, "Strip."

I need very little encouraging at this point in the night, so I reach up to untie the bow around my halter dress and let it slink slowly off my body. I'm so pleased with Ken's reaction I immediately burst into laughter as his jaw drops.

My lingerie is red, lacy, and downright pornographic. A strapless bra lifting my breasts into perfect cleavage matches a belt and panty set connected to thigh-high hose. I waxed every inch of my body below the neck, a fact Ken fully understands when I put one foot up on the bed next to him to reveal that the panties are, in fact, crotchless.

With everything just inches from his face, it isn't long before Ken moves his head forward and kisses my inner thigh, putting his hand behind my ass to bring me closer. His kisses get closer to my pussy, and I laugh as he pulls back for a second, then spins me around so he is now standing above me as I lie on the bed. I ease myself back toward my pillow and wait for him to join me at the top of the bed, but he only has eyes for my wetness as he quickly undresses down to his boxers and crawls back up between my legs.

Maybe it's the champagne or just the relief to be done with such a long day, but I am so giddy I nearly cry as he expertly goes down on me like a pro. His tongue finds my clitoris and flicks and sucks it so much I feel dizzy. His tongue comes in and out of me and the moans he makes are so damn hot. Every once in a while, he'll reach a hand up to squeeze one of my breasts and I revel in how much he is enjoying my body. He uses his fingers to penetrate me over and over again while his tongue still goes to town on my clit and after what feels like the greatest ten minutes of my life, I shudder and have a truly intense orgasm that almost makes me want to sleep.

As he smiles, clearly pleased with himself for making me so happy, his tongue slides a bit lower. Everything feels so great and I am so tipsy that I don't want him to stop. Quickly, he pulls off my panties while I nod and soon, I am wearing only my bra while he continues to explore me with his tongue. I moan in response to his touch. We're hot, sticky, and both just drunk enough to be unabashedly in ecstasy.

"Fuck me," I cry. "Fuck me, fuck me, fuck me."

Ken slides out of me for just a minute and rolls me onto my side. Pressed up behind me, he can now hold on to my tits while he comes out of me, keeping me still while he thrusts in and out and in and out. He even reaches one hand down to my clit to keep me high on that drug and I wonder if I've ever been this aroused before. Everything he does feels right; every instinct is right on point.

"Uhhh" I moan. "More."

And more he does. On and on we go until I can't remember how long we've been going. We finally finish and collapse in a heap on the bed.

It's one of the best nights of sleep I ever had.

Chapter Twenty-Four

February 14

I wake up in Ken's arms, naked, sweaty, and smiling. I look up to see him staring at me and am pleasantly surprised to see his face looking about the same as mine. Well, maybe a bit different.

"What?" I say, as he raises his eyebrows at me in a flirty way.

"I was just trying to decide if you'd like to be woken up with a kiss or a quick fuck, but now you're awake, I suppose you can decide for yourself," he says with a boyish laugh.

Ahh, morning wood. I gently nudge Ken onto his back and climb on top of him to find him completely ready and raring to go. I bend down to kiss him as I take him inside me and say, "Both. I choose both."

With slow, circular movements, I ride him and make quick work of it, remembering from mornings with Carter that it doesn't usually take much to get a man off first thing in the morning. Thinking of Carter while fucking Ken feels super weird and wrong, but I play it off by quickly jumping off once he's done and making my way to the bathroom for a full shower.

When I come out of the bathroom in my delightful hotel robe, I find Ken dressed, smiling, and surrounded by room service and roses. "Happy Valentine's Day," he says, clearly quite pleased with himself.

"How'd you pull this off?" I'm trying to figure out how long I've been in the bathroom.

"Scheduled it all this week." He sounds almost smug. "I ordered everything in advance and set the alarm to wake up just before it all arrived. We woke up just in time. It couldn't have been more perfect. And neither could you."

Well shit, I think, taking the whole scene in. So much for a distraction to the craziness of the Plan. Unless I'm sorely mistaken, Ken is falling for me.

We eat our breakfast in the lazy way only two childless adults can on a Sunday morning, taking time to taste everything on the trays until I'm about ready to climb back in bed for a nap. I'm about to stand up to do just that when Ken jumps up, claps his hands, and says, "Shall we move on to phase two?"

"What's phase two?" I ask, looking longingly at the bed behind him and realizing it's probably not a nap.

"Phase two, my dear, requires us to get dressed and leave this lovely room, but no need to be fancy." He somehow senses I am in no mood for excessive primping.

"Deal." I smile at how excited Ken clearly seems to be.

As I get dressed in the jeans and T-shirt I packed to head home in, I am interrupted mid-ponytail by Ken's hands which guide my hands back down.

"Could you leave your hair down for phase two?" he says, with a pleading look.

Now, my hair is a bit of a mess after not fully being dealt with post-wedding and post-fucking last night, but as I assume I'm heading home before any major plans, I oblige and leave it hanging chaotically all over my head. I throw on my sunglasses as we leave the room, feeling oddly like a celebrity trying to dodge paparazzi as I secretly pray we don't see anyone from the wedding on our way out.

We manage to get to the parking lot unseen and as I walk to my car, I notice Ken beaming. He grins even bigger as I drop my suitcase into my trunk, then he pulls me into a big bear hug and kisses me on the lips. As we finish, I turn back toward my car to get into the driver's seat, but he's now actively leading me away from what I assumed would be our mode of transportation.

"I thought you took an Uber," I say as I throw my keys into my cross-body purse and try to keep up with Mr. Super Excited.

"Yeah, I said that to throw you off," he laughs back.

I'm picturing champagne and strawberries in a limo as we weave through the crowded parking lot when my stomach drops. There, right in front of the hotel, is the motorcycle I remember Ken straddling in the first picture I ever saw of him. It's glistening in the sunlight and looking like a whole heap of oh hell no.

"We're...we're not... Uh, where's your car?" I stammer, involuntarily shaking my head.

"Oh, come on," he pleads. "I have a whole route for us planned and I'm really safe. You'll love it."

I won't love it. Every muscle in my body has now tensed up and my brain is screaming at this suggestion, but Ken continues his case.

"It's such a beautiful time of year and it'll be romantic as hell. You can hold on to me and all you have to do is just look around and enjoy the ride. Plus, I've heard the vibration between your legs is killer foreplay for women."

Okay, that part has me intrigued. And really, it's not like I don't trust Ken to keep me safe. I mean, I don't trust the other drivers on the road not to come crashing into us at eighty miles per hour, but...*stop. Stop right now.* If I keep thinking like this, I'll hurt his feelings. Besides, how far can we possibly be going?

"Hand me a helmet," I say, to his absolute delight.

*

It turns out, we go pretty damn far. What I'm thinking would be just a leisurely ride around town turns into a multi-freeway trip up north to Sedona. Now, Sedona, Arizona, is one of my favorite places in the entire world. The red rocks make for some of the most beautiful views I've ever seen, something I might have been able to enjoy if I hadn't been on the back of the nightmare-machine. Yeah, that's what I call this stupid thing now.

First of all, helmets, while practical, suck to wear for two hours straight. We hit a bit of traffic getting into the main part of Sedona, but instead of using that time to take in the views, I spend it counting the bugs that have splattered onto my visor (eleven) and mentally preparing the speech I am going to give Ken once we finally stop.

As we pull into a parking spot at one of my favorite restaurants, though, I am too distracted to tell Ken just how I feel about this whole thing. He's brought us to Elote Café, a great spot with views of the sunset each night that rivals any location in town. However, not only are we massively underdressed and disheveled by this point, I also know it won't be open because they only serve dinner.

"Huh, that's strange," Ken says as he takes off his helmet. "I figured this place would be popular today."

"Th-they're on-only op-open f-f-for d-dinner," I say shakily as I try to steady myself post-ride.

"Well, shoot." He looks so disappointed I can't bring myself to add "sucks at planning things" to my list of things to chastise him for. "I guess we should hop back on and head somewhere else."

"Actually," I say, getting my voice and balance back. "There are a few places just down the road that should be open. Let's stretch our legs and walk, shall we?"

"Great!" He reaches for my hand.

I am still truly irritated and now dreading the ride home with a vengeance, but I figure some lunch would be a good idea no matter what we end up doing.

"So, what did you think of the ride? Best thing ever, right?"

"Uh..." I'm unable to put into words what my least favorite part was. In addition to the crippling fear I had just from being on the damn bike, I'm now exhausted from holding on to him so tightly that I thought my arms might fall off. "Oooh—they look open," I say, changing the subject and pointing to a little bar and café as we approach it.

A few shots of tequila and a decent lunch later, I begin to feel a bit chattier.

"So, Ken," I begin. "Would you be terribly disappointed if I figured out how to get a ride back home in some sort of car?"

"You hated the bike," he says, dropping his head a bit. "I thought you were digging your arms into me because you were excited."

"Oh no, not excited," I admit. "Pretty terrified the whole way, actually."

"I'm so sorry, honey." He reaches out to grab my hands. "I knew you were uptight, but I thought this day trip might loosen you up a bit."

Uptight? Did he just call me uptight?

"Well, I knew you were an idiot, but I didn't think you were also inconsiderate," I shoot back before I can stop myself.

I know in about a half second that I am way out of line, but I dig my heels in and go full bitch.

"You take me on a motorcycle, something I'm clearly not comfortable with," I say, picking up steam as I go. "Then you take me to a restaurant that's not even open—way to go on that, by the way. And now you have the nerve to sit there and call *me* uptight? Just because I don't want to be on this ridiculous date?"

"Well, if I'm such an idiot," he says, standing up, "then why are you the one stuck here a hundred miles from home and I'm the one leaving you sitting here to pay the bill?"

His words haven't even registered in my ears as my eyes see him storm out of the restaurant, truly leaving me both stranded and in possession of the unpaid check. Just when I think things can't get worse, I reach up to scratch an itch on my arm only to discover it's on fire. I head to the bathroom to discover that not only do I look like a woman about three days into a bender, but I'm also sunburned from the ride up.

I give the woman looking back at me in the mirror, who I can only now see as Binge-drinking Barbie, a dirty look and she shoots it right back. I don't blame her; I don't really like myself so much right now either.

*

I want to tell you I didn't call a boy to come and rescue me from Sedona on Valentine's Day evening. I want to tell you I came up with a brilliant plan to get back home and that I definitely saved some nuns and kittens along the way.

I want to tell you all those things, but alas, I cannot.

I do a quick scan of my best options only to rule Meg out (honeymoon) and also Kim (super pissed at me, and I'm super pissed at her, ugh!). I can't think of anyone else who wouldn't be horrified to come to my rescue, so I text Carter, but he is working and can't get away. That leaves me with Javier, who not only drives up to get me, but could not have been sweeter on the phone with me, explaining he'll be there just as soon as he cleans up after making dinner for his mother.

It was unfair of me to call him, but the sound of his voice immediately gives me so much comfort that I hardly mind watching couple after couple come through the little pavilion I'm waiting in, clearly out for romantic evenings with their significant others, as I sit there looking about as insignificant as I've ever felt. Ken had planned a whole day for us and I'd ruined it. Granted, the plan was not great, but it was a plan nonetheless and I made him feel small. I don't blame him one bit for ditching me and know I'll be eating crow the next time I see him.

When Javier calls me to let me know he is pulling into the parking lot, I do my best to smooth my hair as I walk toward his car. I open the door and sit down, immediately flashing back to the last time I'd been in this exact seat. How different it feels, just two weeks later! But then I look up at Javier and smile to see him looking back at me with genuine concern.

"So, do you want to describe this guy who left you here for me so I don't kick the wrong guy's ass? We can go straight to his house if you like." Javier's tone makes me believe he'd do just that.

"He's not worth it," I reply, realizing immediately what I'd known after the night at the trivia bar. I might not have a clue who I'll end up with at the end of all this, but I one thing is for sure: it won't be Ken.

"So, is Mr. February out of the running then?" he asks hopefully as we pull back onto Highway 89 toward Phoenix.

"I think he is. But I think I need to take the rest of this month to get my head on straight."

I say it quickly, hoping to prevent Javier from asking more questions, but it seems to send him into a thoughtful instead of a talkative mood. We both sit for the next hour lost in our thoughts as we drive back down to the Valley in the dark.

"Remember, Cyn, my offer to kick this guy's ass is on the table," says Javier as we pull in front of my car, still parked outside the hotel. "But I also need to get my head straight at the moment."

He says that last part quickly as I instinctively lean in to kiss him, which is probably for the best. Can't get my head straight if it's right up next to his.

"I'll call you," I say, as I get out of the car. "Maybe not for a little while and hopefully not because I need rescuing again, but there are things that need said."

"Of course." He nods. "Take care of yourself."

And that's just what I plan to do.

Chapter Twenty-Five

www.flavorsofthemonth.bloggerific.com

If you didn't find the love of your life yesterday, make plans to come to our next speed dating event! Heck, I may even sit in on a few rounds to see about finding someone for April because I've now got March all lined up. K and I didn't quite hit it off like I thought we would have, but he's a great guy and I wish him well. For anyone still looking to send in email submissions, here are a few tips:

1. I don't like motorcycles. If you ride them, this isn't a deal breaker, but don't expect me to get on one. Like, ever.

2. Mansplainers need not apply.

If you're cool with both of those stipulations, please feel free to drop me a line. I am not giving up on this plan and still believe my future husband is out there, maybe even reading this blog. Fingers crossed!

FEBRUARY 27

I spent the last two weeks catching up on work, doing kickboxing classes to work off some frustration, and applying aloe to my arms to get through this nasty sunburn. I wake up today finally feeling better when my phone dings with something I wasn't expecting.

Ken: *Kiss and make up?*

Now, I had pretty much assumed I would never hear from Ken again after what will be referred to forever as the Sedona Incident, but I'd rather not carry around anger toward this guy for the rest of my life, so I compose a witty retort.

Me: *Not sure about that first part, but I'm down for the latter.*

Ken: *Be right over.*

As I nervously wait for his arrival, I furiously clean up my kitchen to pass the time. Now, my kitchen wasn't actually dirty, so I mostly just wipe my counter over and over again, but it feels productive and that's what matters.

Ken knocks on my door with three quick knocks. I decide this does not sound aggressive or angry, so I answer the door to find a sheepish Ken mirroring the same face I think I'm making. We both let out a small laugh and I let him hug me and kiss me on the cheek as he crosses the threshold.

We sit on my couch for about a minute before both blurting out something at the same time. I know mine is an apology and his sounds like one, too, but I nod to him to let him say his piece.

"I'm so sorry," he says. "For everything."

"I am too," I say. "For all the things."

Hey, if he can be vague, so can I. We both smile and relax back into our seats until he sits up a bit straighter to talk again.

"I hope you don't mind, but I called your friend Kim for advice."

As that was about the last thing I thought he'd say, I sit gaping at him until he goes on.

"She said you really can be stubborn and awful sometimes. But that you're also very loving and she's sure you're falling for me."

Now, I don't really enjoy being insulted under the guise of a compliment, but the thing I'm most fixated on is Kim's weird advice that I am falling for Ken. We haven't spoken since what will forever be known as the Wedding Slut-Shaming Incident, but I know she didn't think I was falling for this guy. What is she playing at?

Realizing I can't fight battles on two fronts, I instead try to think of how to let Ken down gently from this weird relationship precipice we now find ourselves facing. Here he is, thinking we can work it out and here I am, thinking *dude please leave*. I decide to go with an honest approach, while hopefully letting him down gently.

"Ken, I…"

He'll never know what I was going to say, and I kinda forget as well, as he is soon kissing me with the sweetest kiss we've shared. It isn't urgent in the way I know he can kiss when he is dying to get me naked, but it does have an undercurrent of something I can't quite name.

I should pull away and tell him he definitely isn't the one. And if he isn't the one, I definitely shouldn't let him stay the night, while he hopes to win me back.

"What if this isn't meant to be?" I whisper, feeling like at least raising the concept might be enough to get me off the hook from any post-coital guilt.

"Then we'll have one last night to remember this by," he whispers back, pulling me onto his lap and pressing my body against his.

I soon forget to care that I know we'll never end up together. Ken cares for me and either doesn't seem bothered that we aren't meant for each other, or truly believes that one night of sex might be enough to make me fall in love with him. Either way, it would be cruel to send him home now. Right? Yeah, I'm going to tell myself that's right.

We're still just kissing when Ken puts both hands on my ass and lets out a moan. I flash back to our drunken sexcapade after the wedding and my cheeks flush as I remember how much I'd enjoyed it all then. I know then there's no way I'm letting this guy leave tonight and judging by the bulge I'm now gyrating on, I don't think that will be a problem.

We both stand up to remove the clothes that are now inconveniently in the way of things we'd like to be doing and sit back down in the same position we'd been in with our clothes on. We haven't worked our way up to anything nearly as much as I'd like, but Ken whispers, "Don't worry—this is just round one," into my ear as I slide myself onto him slowly. We're just getting going when he says, "Who's an idiot now?" and I nearly fall off.

He pulls me back to center, thrusts a few times with his eyes closed, and climaxes faster than I can say "what the what now?"

I can't think of a normal way to ask him what the fuck that was about while he's still inside me, so I stand up, head to the bathroom to clean up, splash some water on my face, and head back to have what I can only assume will be the most awkward conversation in history.

But then I see him and I realize that I do, on some level, kinda think he's an idiot. It has less to do with him and everything to do with me, but it's there and I can't shake it. Once you have labeled a potential suitor, how do you undo it with a quickie and the world's weirdest mid-coital question? But just because my bitchy, judgmental brain will always now see Ken as a sexy, dumb, sweet guy, I see no reason to hurt his feelings.

"Here's the thing, Ken," I begin.

"I'm not the One," he finishes.

"You're not."

"Yeah, I don't really think you are, either. I mean, I think you're great and all, but I just don't see it."

I want to protest, wondering how he could go so quickly from trying to win me back into full-on surrender, but I realize that in the same way I can never see him differently, he'll never be able to see me as anyone other than the woman who called him an idiot. And I don't blame him.

I let Ken wrap me up in one of his amazing hugs, and we both just kind of stand there for a minute. It's not bad, as far as breakups go, but it's still an emotional moment. I hurt a nice guy's feelings and I'll need to carry that with me through this whole process. I'm about to apologize once again to truly clear the air between us when Ken pulls away from me with a weird look in his eyes.

"But what if we're wrong?" he says, gazing at me with an intensity that is kinda freaking me out.

"About what?" I say, worried that we're about to have a much worse breakup.

My words are barely out when Ken's eyes light up and he drops to one knee in front of me.

Holy fucking shit.

"I'm just kidding." Ken jumps back up off his knee. "It was getting a bit too serious in here and I thought we could use a laugh."

"Oh!" I say, recovering from a mild heart attack. "Ha-ha-ha-ha-ha-ha-ha-ha."

I hope my laugh doesn't sound fake, but Ken seems fine with it, so I must be doing okay.

"Mind if I crash here tonight?" he says. "I'd love to just hold you one more night."

I can't tell if he's kidding and now think he's super crazy, but I nod, and we head back down the hall to my room. He falls asleep quickly and I manage to eventually doze off after sneaking out to take a sleeping pill. For anyone keeping score at home, that's three pseudo-proposals in as many months and I'll be damned if that's not completely bananas. Even if this last one was really not a proposal *at all,* I had about twenty seconds of sheer panic and settling down for the night without drugs is just not going to happen.

Chapter Twenty-Six

February 28

Ken slipped away sometime early this morning without saying goodbye and that's just fine by me. To be fair, he might have said goodbye and I just didn't hear it, as Carter used to tell me I would sleep through his kiss when he'd leave early for school or the gym. I pause for a minute to think longingly about Carter's kisses before jumping out of bed to face the day.

Even though I never had any intention of falling in love this month, I didn't expect to find myself even more confused now than I was in the aftermath of Javier's faux proposal. Did the fact I assumed I wouldn't fall for Ken cause me to look for reasons to not like/love him? Is my brain that powerful?

I decide here and now to stay open to the possibility of love with Peter and each guy going forward. I'm pretty sure nothing could have saved Ken and me from total destruction, but just in case, I'd rather not jinx anything. So for today, it's time to close the book on Ken and watch romantic comedies to help get ready for March.

Chapter Twenty-Seven

March 1

It is the dawn of a new era, y'all. I honestly can't see straight whenever I think about this mess I've gotten myself into, so I have also made the resolution to *slow the fuck down*. Literally. I am going to wait and really get to know my next ten suitors—and yes, I'm including Carter here—before having sex with them. It's the sex that is screwing everything up. Also literally. Ha-ha. I really crack myself up sometimes.

If I had waited to sleep with Ken, I don't think I ever would have been confused about my feelings for him. As great as we were together physically, we simply weren't compatible emotionally and I almost can't believe I didn't see it sooner. So, as I get ready to revisit an old crush this month, I feel like it's only fair to give us a proper chance. Can you even imagine how cool it would be to end up with the guy I dreamed about in high school? Sixteen-year-old me is downright giddy at the thought of it.

Slowing down with my guys should also hopefully give me some time to fix things with my girls. Meg is back from her honeymoon, and we are getting together tomorrow night to catch up. And by catch up, I of course mean I will need to do some serious groveling for allowing my and Kim's drama to get in the way of her beautiful wedding. Speaking of Kim, she's officially not returning any of my calls or texts, so I can only wonder what she's feeling about this whole thing. I know better than to push her to talk until she's ready, but I can't shake the feeling that I'm unsteady in this whole thing without her.

Thus, Meg-less and Kim-less, I instead fill Samantha, my assistant, in on everything that's been going on as we enjoy smoothies after a spin class this morning.

"So, Ken's a 'no,' but Javier and Carter are still in the running," she says, recapping our conversation thus far.

"Exactly." I sip my smoothie a bit too fast and give myself brain freeze.

"And this new guy is someone you've liked since basically forever?"

"Basically, yes."

"So, are you taking him to the Prom?" she asks, raising her

eyebrows in excitement.

"Holy frijoles," I say, realizing what she means. "That's this month, isn't it?"

The Prom she's referring to isn't quite like the one we had in high school. Put on every March by a local charity, it's a great night for adults to get all dressed up while supporting a fantastic cause. Sinfully Good always participates by sponsoring the dessert table, and this year, Samantha and I will both be attending.

I'm suddenly elated that I get to go to Prom with Peter Donavan, and I make a mental note to wait to sleep with him until that night. It'll be just like in high school where half the girls in my class lost their virginity on prom night! Except I'm not a virgin, and they probably weren't either. So, I guess it is about the same.

"Can I throw something out there that you might hate?" Samantha says.

"You may," I say, trying to think of a worse way to introduce a new idea and failing.

"What if we get the public more involved in your process? You know, thousands of people are already reading your blog posts and I think it could be really great for business. You could probably get a lot of free press if you wouldn't mind a few cameras on your dates with these guys."

"No way." I shake my head and shudder at the thought. "This is hard enough without any extra pressure. I don't mind the blog coverage and I'm glad people are interested, but the whole point of this is that the stores are already doing well. I need this to be just about me. And twelve guys. You know what I mean."

"Of course," she says. "Forget I mentioned it."

We're done with our smoothies, so I head home to write a new blog post and make plans with Peter. I've got to give him plenty of time to find a tux before the prom rolls around.

Chapter Twenty-Eight

www.flavorsofthemonth.bloggerific.com

Well, it's March and you know what that means, friends—madness. I'm very excited to embark on this month's dating extravaganza because it's actually someone I knew from high school. Don't tell him, but I had a huge crush on him back in the day. With that in mind, I've been toying around in the kitchen and came up with the perfect flavor—Cookie Crush Supreme! Basically, I smashed some Oreos and messed with some of my favorite flavors until I was happy with how it turned out. It's a good rule for life, really: when all else fails, add some cookies and keep moving forward until everything works out.

Don't forget: the Valley Youth Initiative Prom is coming up in a few weeks and Sinfully Good will be there as always. Tickets are still available, and you can help us keep local kids safe and healthy by attending or donating any time at one of our stores.

Have you been to one of our speed dating parties? Met anyone interesting? Email us here and fill us in on how it's going! We'd love it if any connections from this fun idea turns into something great. Until then, enjoy this month of Spring Training, perfect weather, and March Madness for any of you who are into that sort of thing. Personally, I'd take baseball over basketball any day, but even I'll admit those brackets make everything a bit more exciting. Even if I do just pick whichever team has the better mascot in my opinion. And yes, that's exactly what I do.

MARCH 2

"I'm not sure what else to say."

I'm looking at Meg with eyes full of contrition, hoping she understands how much I care for her and how I am hoping she can forgive me.

"It's okay," she says. "I don't think too many people realized you guys were actually fighting, and the ones who did just thought it was funny. We may never get my nephew to stop saying the word 'slut,' but he was bound to pick it up on the streets eventually."

I throw my head back in laughter and realize how good it feels to do just that. I'd been worried for weeks that Meg would be mad forever and I certainly wouldn't have blamed her, but here she is not only forgiving me but easing any tension I feel with laughter.

"I still haven't heard from Kim," I say, addressing the elephant in the room.

"I know," she says. "That's why I arranged for you both to sit down and talk next week."

"You pushy bitch," I tease.

"You ignorant slut," she fires back, a reference to a great *SNL* bit that she knows I love.

"Are you at least going to fill me in on why she's mad at me?" I ask, knowing full well I'm not going to get much out of her.

"I might if I even understood it fully myself," she says, and I believe her. "I thought it was because she's just not happy in her own love life and here you are with multiple options, but it's definitely more than that."

"I'd say so."

We move quickly from the friend drama and into a honeymoon recap that makes me so happy for Meg and Fred. Not only are they great friends who love to see the world together, but they also have so much passion for each other that I can see her love for him radiating as she fills me in. This is it. This is what I want.

"So, did you have sex every day? Twice a day?" I say, pressing her as only a true friend can about the best parts of the honeymoon.

"Every day and then some." She turns scarlet as she looks away from me. "It was amazing."

"Any details you'd like to share?" I raise my eyebrows as I try to coax a bit more out of her.

"Well, there was this one night where we had sex on a catamaran on the way back from a snorkeling trip, but then the rest of the people on the boat complained and we had to stop," she says with a completely straight face.

"*Really*?"

"No." She laughs at the look on my face. "But we definitely thought about it."

Chapter Twenty-Nine

March 7

Who says you can't go home again? I'm about to go on a date with Peter Donavan. *Peter Donovan*! You guys! He was the cutest guy at my high school and I always wanted to go on a date with him and now I get to. My butterflies have butterflies. I'm pacing around my apartment waiting for him to pick me up when the doorbell rings and I almost scream.

I hurry to the door and there he is. Tall, brooding, and delicious. Peter Fucking Donavan.

We're heading to a Spring Training baseball game today in Scottsdale, so I went for sporty chic, and I laugh as I realize we're wearing opposing team attire. Whereas I've got on my Arizona Diamondbacks tank top and hat, Peter is decked out in Los Angeles Dodgers gear.

"I thought you were a Dodgers fan," he says, as I invite him inside.

"Oh no, I hate those guys," I say, before realizing I might be insulting his team.

He laughs and gives a sigh of relief. "Oh good. I just wore this to impress you. I can't stand those guys. But I could have sworn you were a Dodgers fan back in high school."

I love that he tried to remember who I liked, but who wears the jersey of a rival team to impress a girl? Not a real D-backs fan, for one. I'm trying to think of why he'd think I was a Dodgers fan, but then he leans down to kiss me and I can't even remember my name. You guys. Peter Donavan is kissing me. With his *tongue*. I just got to first base with Peter Donavan!

"Sorry," he says, as he pulls away from me. "I've just wanted to do that for about fifteen years."

"Don't apologize," I say, as I catch my breath. "I've been wanting the same thing."

I step on my tiptoes to kiss him again. But this time, the shock of the first kiss has worn off and I realize I'm about to break my new Slow Down rule. Sure, I know Peter…sort of. I'm not sure we really talked much in high school, though, so that probably doesn't count. But here we are kissing in my entryway, and I feel like a teenager again. By which, of course, I mean horny and super excited that our parents aren't around to walk in on us. Peter slides his hands down my back to my ass, and I realize we're never going to make it to the game at this rate.

"So hey," I say as I pull away from him. "What do you say we get you changed out of those Dodgers clothes and into a D-backs jersey?"

"Good call," he says, and we head out of the door, leaving all thoughts of getting it on behind us. For now.

As we walk down to where he's parked his car, another rush of teenage hormonal nostalgia washes over me. There it is: Peter's Mustang. I always wanted to take a ride in his car when we went to school together and now I get to. Me! Cynthia Blake! I'm secretly hoping one of our friends from school will see us on our way to the game when he starts the engine and it barely sputters to life.

"Should we take my car?" I ask, now wondering if we'll even make it to the game in this car.

"No way," he says. "She just needs a minute to warm up and then we're good to go. This car is my baby."

*

There's something about sitting in the grass on a sunny day watching baseball that is just so damn sexy. We grab a few beers during the game as we sit on a blanket in left field and even though it's warm and I know I'm covered in sweat, we can't keep our hands off each other. It's pretty much nine innings of foreplay, as all baseball games should be, really. For the last three innings, I sit between Peter's legs and lean back against his strong body. Every few minutes, he'll kiss my neck or shoulders and I'll give out an involuntary moan.

In denim shorts and a scoop-neck tank top, I have to say I am in prime sexy/sporty territory, and I take every opportunity available to flaunt it. Whether I am lying on my stomach and looking up at Peter as he comes back with more beers or throwing my head back to laugh while I lean against him, there are plenty of opportunities for him to gaze at my ample cleavage. And gaze he does.

We spend the game reminiscing about friends we had in common back in the day, or Peter does, anyway. I can't remember most of the people he mentions, but I don't want to remind him that I wasn't terribly cool when we were in school, so I just nod along. I'll look back in my yearbook tomorrow and figure out who he was talking about, but I don't want to spoil the day. We don't connect emotionally, but I've been waiting to sleep with this guy for almost half of my life. Surely the Slow Down pact has contingencies in place for situations like this?

I know Peter is on the same page, too, when one of the kisses he plants on my neck in the bottom of the ninth lingers a bit longer.

"Your boobs are all sweaty," he says in a low whisper. "We should probably get you to the showers."

"But coach," I say back. "What if I need your help reaching all over my body?"

"Fuuuuuuuuuuuuck me. Baby, I'd be more than happy to help."

As we stumble out of the stadium, tipsy, sweaty, and giddy with desire, we both realize we shouldn't be driving. I'm semi-relieved to not have to get back in his car as we grab a cab back to his apartment, which isn't far from the stadium.

In the backseat, we lazily make out, both a little drowsy from all the beer and sunshine. As we pull up to his apartment complex, I realize how close we are to our old school.

"I didn't realize you still live in the old neighborhood," I say as we get out of the cab.

"Oh yeah," he replies. "It's easier for the guys and me this way."

It takes me a second to process what he's saying, but as we walk up the stairs to his apartment, I hear voices shouting on the inside and it dawns on me: Peter has roommates.

Now, there's nothing wrong with roommates, per se. But as I take in the scene in the living room, I immediately flash back to high school. It's Peter's three best friends from school sitting on a couple of couches and bean bags playing a video game together. I know immediately that this exact scenario took place repeatedly back in the '90s and can't help but wonder if those are even the same couches a few girls I went to school with lost their virginity on. Ick.

"Guys, you remember Cyn, right?" Peter says as we walk in.

"Oh yeah—hey there," the one on the left says. It's Justin something-or-other. I'm pretty sure Meg had a crush on him back in the day. I wonder what she'll think when I tell her he still wears the same No Fear shirt.

"Do you want to go back to my place?" I say hopefully, turning quickly around and realizing I'm a bit dizzy.

"Nah, we're already here," says Peter. "And besides, didn't I promise to help you shower?"

I know there is no way I'm going to want to take a shower with these other guys in the apartment. Heck, I don't really want to pee here where everyone can hear me, let alone have sex for the first time with an old crush.

"Oh, uh, let's go to your room and talk first," I say.

"Sure thing," he says. "It's this way."

As he takes my hand and walks me down the hall to the back bedroom, I get glimpses of the other rooms and shudder. It's like time has stood still and not one of these boys ever learned how to clean his room. I am immediately sympathetic toward and pissed at their moms for not teaching them better. We get to Peter's room, and it's thankfully the cleanest of the bunch. I also see that he has his own bathroom and feel slightly better, but still not great.

As soon as we close the door, Peter is kissing me and clumsily fumbling with my tank top.

"You are so hot," he slurs into the side of my face. "I can't believe we're finally doing this."

He's drunk and my temporary judgmental sobriety has passed, so I sink back into a tipsy stupor with him. I take a step back so I can remove my baseball hat and I do that sexy move where I pull my hair out of the ponytail, shake it loose, and totally wow him. The only problem is that I really was sweaty, so I can feel it falling a bit flat, but I quickly pull my tank top off to distract Peter. It works and he rushes toward me again to kiss me as we fall back onto his bed.

I'm still in shorts and my bra and Peter is fully dressed, but we make out furiously as only two drunk people can. I wrap my legs around him and pull us closer together. It's hot as hell, but something isn't quite right. We roll to the side and as Peter reaches to pull his shirt off, I reach down between his legs to turn him on some more. Only, instead of finding him hard and ready to go, I find him…not so ready to go. I move my hand a bit more encouragingly and Peter gives an awkward laugh.

"It must have been all the beer," he says. "Mind if we just rest for a minute?"

"Oh sure," I say, realizing it's silly to expect him to perform when he's drunk and exhausted. In fact, a little cat nap sounds perfect. I nuzzle myself into his arms and quickly fall asleep on his chest.

*

I wake up alone in Peter's bed after the sun has gone down, and it takes me a second to realize where I am. When I hear a bunch of guys yelling from the other room, I realize Peter has joined them in whatever video game they were playing earlier. I find my shirt and use the bathroom so I can freshen up.

As I catch a glimpse of myself in the mirror, I realize I need more than just freshening up. Somewhere between sweating at the game and snuggling on Peter's chest, my makeup has either been completely removed or smudged into different places. My hair is a mess and I'm puffy and swollen from all the beer. I have no desire to be seen by a group of guys I went to high school with, so I evaluate my options. I could shower here and try to make a graceful exit, but a quick peek into Peter's shower reveals only boy products and I don't feel like subjecting my hair to 99-cent shampoo.

Behind me in the mirror's reflection, I notice a window above Peter's bed. It's pretty big and the tree outside it looks sturdy. Why not continue with the day's high school theme and make a break for it? I can't decide if this is childish or brilliant, but then remember I don't actually care.

I throw my hair back in the baseball hat, grab my phone, and open the window. Looking down, I second guess myself for a minute, as the thought of breaking a limb climbing out of a guy's apartment window feels like just about the worst way to injure oneself at this age, or any age really. Maybe it's the leftover beer swirling around in my belly and my brain, but I again push those thoughts aside and throw my leg onto the windowpane.

I easily grab the closest branch with my arm and pull myself completely out of the window. I've got a decent grip on the branch, but don't quite have my footing on the branch below until I kick off my flip-flops and get my balance. From there, I lower myself onto that branch and swing myself down until my legs are dangling what feels like two or three feet from the ground. I decide to just drop and fall in a heap into the wet grass below me.

When I land, I do a quick check and decide I'm not hurt, so I begin to hunt for my flip-flops. Just then, I hear a chuckle to my left and realize I've been spotted by someone.

Praying I won't see Peter or one of his friends when I look up, I raise my gaze until the source of the laughter comes into view. It's a man sitting on the patio of his apartment, which is apparently directly below Peter's. The light is on in his apartment behind him, so I can't see his face, but I quickly put my fingers to my lips to give him the universal sign for "please don't tell your neighbor that you saw me escape his apartment by climbing down a tree."

"Your secret is safe with me," he says, still chuckling to himself. "And here." He extends his arm toward me. "This fell on my head."

It's my flip-flop, I realize. I kicked it off and it hit this guy in the head. I. Am. Mortified.

"Uh, thanks." I get closer and take the shoe he's offering. I can't look him in the eye, but I catch a quick glimpse of black hair, glasses, and a friendly smile. I am in no mood to meet someone right now, so I quickly turn around and make a break for the front of the apartment complex as I request an Uber to pick me up. Somehow, I feel like high school me would not be super proud of how my first date with Peter

Donavan went.

*

I wake up this morning with a bruised ego and a couple of scrapes on my knees, but not bad considering I fell out of a tree last night with all the grace of a drunken dock worker. I am immediately relieved and confused that my explanation to Peter worked like a charm.

Peter: *Uh, where are you?*

Me: *I left a few minutes ago. You said goodbye to me, remember?*

Peter: *Oh yeah, sorry. I thought you were just getting something from your car.*

Now, my car wasn't at his complex, and neither is his for that matter, but I'll let him sort that out later. We set a date for later this week to get dinner and see a play, which should be a much better date than our beer-buzzed first try. I keep cringing thinking about yesterday, but it's not like I made a super great impression, so there's no sense judging him. I'm also way behind at work, so I turn my attention to my inbox and soon I'm lost in a budget spreadsheet with no thoughts of trees, beer, flip-flops hitting strangers… Okay, I'm still thinking about it a little bit.

We've had a great response to our first few speed dating events, so I've got to get another one scheduled. As I open my calendar, I also see I'm supposed to have lunch with Kim tomorrow, and my stomach is immediately tied in knots.

Here's what I know about Kim:

1. Something about my relationship with Javier made her angry.

2. Something about this whole plan made her angry.

3. She completely shuts down when she is angry.

4. Except when she is calling me a slut in front of hundreds of people.

5. I really don't want to see her tomorrow.

6. Yes, I do. I miss her.

I decide to break the ice for tomorrow with a quick text to confirm plans.

Me: *Are we still on for lunch at Kierland?*

Kim: *Actually, something came up. Raincheck?*

Me: *Really? Can you reschedule the other thing?*

Kim: *I really can't. I'm sorry. But I promise I'll see you soon.*

So much for burying the hatchet. I both can and can't believe she would bail on me. I feel our friendship slipping away and that scares the shit out of me. I don't want to drag Meg back into this and the only other person I can think to talk to about it is Carter, which also seems wrong because he's not too happy with me either.

Instead, I turn my attention to my inbox to see that I'm way behind on email submissions.

Dear Cynthia,

I think you and I could really hit it off. Your blog post about Gilmore Girls really resonated with me and I think I could be the Jess to your Rory. In fact, my name is actually Jess, so we're already halfway there. Maybe you could change your name? Kidding.

I'm thirty-three and very interested in meeting you. I also own my own business and think it's great that you've done so well with your stores. I'm writing to you now because I'm excited about your Plan, but I'll actually be gone most of April on a service trip to Central America. Could we kick things off in May?

Sincerely, Jess

Well, now, that's a great letter right there. A fellow business owner who is also dedicated to philanthropy? And a guy who loves *Gilmore Girls*? I take about three seconds to think it over before hitting the reply button.

Dear Jess,

I'd love to meet you in May. Be safe on your trip and call me when you get home. I'm open to the name change, ha-ha.

Sincerely,

Cynthia (Rory)

I read through the next few submissions, deleting the one about the guy who thinks I'm going to hell for dating too many guys. To be fair, he said there's a chance I could still get to Heaven if I let him give me his testament, but I'm gonna pass on that offer. I also deleted several that included unsolicited dick pics (because ew) and one from a gentleman who is twice my age (because also ew). I'm still keeping an eye out for an April contender, but since no other messages are catching my eye just yet, I decide to focus back on the month at hand.

Chapter Thirty

March 10

After a really nice dinner at Hanny's in Downtown Phoenix, Peter and I are grabbing a glass of wine during intermission at *Rent*. I've seen it about twenty times and know the soundtrack by heart, but it's Peter's first time and I'm happy to see him enjoying it.

"Didn't you do all the shows when we were in high school?" he says, putting an arm around me as we walk through the lobby.

"Oh, er, no," I say awkwardly. "I tried a couple of times and was in the company freshman and sophomore year, but it turns out I'm not as talented as I thought I was."

"I must have just noticed you in the background," he says kindly.

I'm not sure how, but I like that he remembers me that way. I literally played a Munchkin in *The Wizard of Oz* and hope that's not the mental picture he's had of me all these years, but it's still sweet.

Our conversation at dinner flows nicely and I'm glad to see our first date chaos doesn't seem to be the norm for him. As excited as I was for our first date, Peter seems to be even more excited to be out with me! If only I'd had the courage to tell him how I felt in high school, we might have been one of those couples who marries their high school sweethearts and lives happily ever after. That happens, right?

I find out that Peter still works at the same place he did when we were in high school (a gym), but he's a personal trainer/manager now and acts as a sort of mentor to the high school kids on his staff.

"I really screwed around back in the day and I'm pretty lucky to have landed on my feet," he confesses over dinner. "And I know it probably seems juvenile to still be hanging with the same group of guys from high school, but those guys are my brothers, and I wouldn't be here without them."

"Wow." I see our previous date in a whole new light. "That's so great that you're always there for each other."

"Always. We might goof around from time to time, but we're all now getting to the point where it's time to settle down and I think they're really rooting for us."

He is smiling at me so earnestly now that I blush, and as I'm wondering if he can see my cheeks flush, I notice his are turning a bit pink as well. So here we sit, a decade and then some after high school, feeling those same feelings from back then. The nostalgia is so thick between us that you could brush it away with your hands. It feels wonderful.

After the show, at which he held my hand all the way through the second act, Peter drives me home while we chat about our favorite parts. He's not a huge theater fan himself, but the fact he clearly seems to have enjoyed it is a great sign, I'd say. As we pull up to my house, I'm doing battle in my head, trying to decide if I should invite him up or keep going with the take it slow plan. As he puts the car in park, I've pretty much decided to abandon the idea when he proposes something even better.

"Want to make out in the back seat?" he says with a boyish grin on his face.

"Oh, heck yes," I say, unbuckling as quickly as I can.

We get into position in record time and begin furiously kissing. It's different this time, now that we're both not sloppily drunk, and it's like I'm sixteen again in an instant. We're parked in front of my condo and there's no one around, but just the thought we might be seen by someone adds an edge to the night that makes me giggle between kisses.

"Worried your dad might come out and tell us to break it up?" he says, laughing into my hair.

"Something like that," I say before pressing my mouth against his again.

There's not a ton of room back here and no possible way this could lead to sex, which I decide is pretty perfect, considering my Prom Plan that I was about to completely ignore ten minutes ago.

"Hey." I realize I haven't shared this plan with him yet. "Would you be my date for the Prom?"

"That charity ball all the fancy people go to?" he says, taking a minute to catch his breath.

"Yeah," I say shyly, now wondering if I'm making him uncomfortable.

"I'll have the prettiest date there. I'd love to."

"I was thinking we could maybe go all the way that night," I add, hoping he'll catch my meaning.

"So, I shouldn't try too much tonight, you mean?"

"I'm not sure how you could back here," I fire back, laughing at how cramped we are.

"Well," he says, "maybe not all the way, but I had a couple ideas."

I raise one eyebrow at him, wondering what he has in mind, but he quickly kisses me before I can think too long about it. As we kiss, his hands begin to caress my breasts, and I realize there's definitely plenty we can do back here that teenage me is super thrilled about. He reaches back to unhook my bra, and I do the supercool thing where I take it off while still wearing my shirt. My blouse is thin, and with my nipples erect, the effect is pretty damn hot.

Peter looks down and smiles. "Any idea how many nights I went to bed dreaming of seeing those?" he asks.

"No, but you're more than welcome to see them now," I say.

Peter reaches down to pull my blouse over my head and gives a grateful sigh. I laugh and throw my head back while he takes the opportunity to touch them first with his hands and then his mouth. It's so damn fun being desired and appreciated like this that I almost forget something about what he said is a bit odd. I love that he said he fantasized about my boobs back in high school, but I didn't really have boobs back then. I mean, maybe he's the kind of guy who fantasizes about an A cup? I guess that's it.

We're both so lost in the heat of the moment that I nearly scream when I hear a knock on the window. The windows are completely steamed up by this point, but I can still make out the shape of a man peering into the car. I pull my shirt in front of me to cover myself while Peter says, "Shit—wait here," and hops out of the car.

I can't hear everything, but it sounds like one of my neighbors thought he was catching a couple of high school kids and is shocked to see a grown man come out of the car. They share a few awkward sentences back and forth until Peter pops back in to say, "You have some nosy-ass people next door."

I have since put my shirt back on, so I grab my bra and get out of the car, grateful that the guy who caught us isn't still right there to see which of his neighbors was making out in the backseat.

"Even if we were a couple of kids," continues Peter, "why does he think he can just interrupt us?"

"Don't know," I say, with a mix of embarrassment and irritation.

"Hey." Peter wraps his arms around me. "Don't worry about it. We'll laugh about it tomorrow. Let me just walk you to your door."

I do just that and give him a quick kiss before heading inside. I can't say for certain, but I feel like I'm being watched the whole way to my house, and it really gives me the creeps. I decide to watch an episode of *Friends* before bed to clear my head and end up falling asleep on the couch.

Chapter Thirty-One

www.flavorsofthemonth.bloggerific.com

I watched The One with the Cat, an episode of Friends, last night and am excited to report that my current situation is not at all like Monica's. For those of you who don't know every episode of Friends by the title (aka normal people), this is the episode where Monica goes on a date with a guy named Chip from high school. Specifically, Chip is Rachel's ex-boyfriend who ditched her at the Prom. Monica is thrilled to be dating a boy who was once out of her league, but quickly realizes he hasn't matured at all, and she gets to be the one to dump him.

It made me laugh, but also made me feel really great about my March flavor, who is every bit as cute as I remember him from high school, but nothing like Chip. We've both grown up nicely and I'm kicking myself for not approaching him back in the day to say hello. So, if you have your eye on someone, speak up! You might not have to wait thirteen years like I did to get back in touch.

MARCH 15

For date number three, Peter and I decide to go out for pizza and games and spend hours playing at a local Dave and Buster's with his friends. We play Skee-Ball for at least an hour, somehow turning the whole thing into a tournament because his friends are super competitive, but I hold my own and come in second place. Between the drinks and laughs all around the arcade floor, I feel like I'm floating all night.

On top of that, his friends all really seem to like me! I guess I probably shouldn't care so much about that, but his friends are such a big part of his life that their approval is almost a prerequisite to date him. Judging by how impressed they are with the number of tickets I win, I'd say I'm in.

While we wait for everyone to join us after work, I ask Peter my apparently traditional set of questions. As he's now the third guy to answer them, I think this is something I'll keep up for the next nine.

1. Given the choice of anyone in the world, who would you want

as a dinner guest? (Peter says Tom Hanks and that's about as lovely an answer as I can think of. He really loves movies like I do and just thinks Tom Hanks is the best thing ever. I can't argue and we ended up discussing our favorite Hanks movies. I tell him I didn't think I could choose between *Sleepless in Seattle* and *A League of Their Own*. Peter says *Toy Story* and I give him a quick kiss for being adorable.)

2. Would you like to be famous? In what way? (Yes, Peter says he'd definitely like to be famous, especially if he were also rich. His job at the gym doesn't pay well and he's tired of not having enough money to be able to travel and do everything he'd like to do. I'm not sure why he'd need to be rich to be famous, but he clearly links the two, so I guess that's that.)

3. Before making a telephone call, do you ever rehearse what you are going to say? Why? (He turns his head at this and says he can't imagine ever doing it. "To be honest, I don't like talking on the phone. I text. I'd rather never talk on the phone again in my life." Well, all right then. I assure him he's a perfectly nice conversationalist, but he says he'd just rather talk to people in person. He's pretty great to look at, so I see no reason to argue.)

4. What would constitute a "perfect" day for you? ("A picnic at the park with everyone playing volleyball, eating good food, and just hanging all day," says Peter. He loves when his friends all come together with their families at the park by our high school to have fun. They apparently actually do this every few months, and I think it's nice

he gets to live his perfect day so often.)

5. When did you last sing to yourself? To someone else? (Peter says he's been known to rock a few songs at karaoke. I point out there's a karaoke stage not far from here. I dare him to show me what he can do. He chuckles and says, "We'll see." Not quite sure how to take that, but I'm intrigued.)

6. If you were able to live to the age of ninety and retain either the mind or body of a thirty-year-old for the last sixty years of your life, which would you want? (Being a physical trainer, I expect Peter to say body, but he says he'd rather retain his mind. Then he adds that since he knows how to stay fit, he'd be able to work out and stay pretty healthy anyway, so it's the best of both worlds. It's sort of cheating, but whatever.)

7. Do you have a secret hunch about how you will die? (Peter laughs and says it will probably be doing a stupid stunt with his friends because they've already come close a few times. I remember hearing about their antics in high school and hope that's what he's referring to, but something tells me they still act like idiots together every once in a while.)

8. Name three things you and your partner appear to have in common. (Peter says we are both friendly, healthy, and… He can't think of another one. He doesn't seem upset by this but says he's still getting to know me and isn't sure what else there is yet. I can think of a few, but I suppose he's right about getting to know each other.)

9. For what in your life do you feel most grateful? ("My friends," says Peter. Not a shocking answer, as he brings them up constantly. I start humming *Wannabe* by the Spice Girls in my head, wondering if that's his go-to song at karaoke. God, I hope so. I can just hear him and the guys crooning, "If you wanna be my lover, you gotta get with my friends." That would be hilarious. And weird. Why am I picturing this?)

10. If you could change anything about the way you were raised, what would it be? (Peter says he wishes he'd had siblings, but otherwise thinks his parents did a pretty great job. I comment that he found his own siblings and he nods, smiling at me sincerely. I get this guy.)

11. Take four minutes and tell your partner your life story in as much detail as possible. (Here, we get into some really deep territory, and I see Peter as so much more than my former crush. He's a sweet, sensitive guy who grew up shy and even a bit awkward. He started getting into working out because he was bullied in junior high. I didn't know him then, so it's hard for me to picture him as a scrawny and scared teenager. By the time I saw him in high school, he was strong and confident. His friends who are so dear to him had similar struggles and they bonded in the weight rooms and while playing video games. It's so different to hear about a boy having a tough adolescence and I'm immediately taken with how open and honest he's being with me. I get the feeling he'd be a really great father, and the thought makes me

smile as I listen to him. This could be the start of something really, really great.)

12. If you could wake up tomorrow having gained any one quality or ability, what would it be? (Peter says he'd like to be able to travel through time so he could go back to when we were in high school and ask me out. I concur.)

On our way out of Dave and Buster's, I stop to use the bathroom. When I come back out, I don't see Peter, but his friends are standing together near a table in the bar area. They're crowding around the table awkwardly and I stop on my way to them, wondering if I'm not meant to see what they're doing. I'm about three feet away from their turned backs when they abruptly part to reveal Peter standing behind them, somehow holding a microphone.

"You never close your eyes anymore when I kiss your lips," he sings, slightly off-key, which might be on purpose, as he's clearly doing his best Tom Cruise as Maverick in *Top Gun* impression.

"And there's no tenderness like before in your fingertips," adds Justin, taking on the role of Goose.

"You're trying hard not to show it, *baby,*" sings Peter, joined by the rest of the guys on that last word and the rest of the phrase.

"Cuz baby I know it. You've lost that loving feeling…"

"Told you I do some pretty great karaoke," he says, letting his backup singers continue without him.

"That. Was. Amazing," I say. "I've always wanted someone to reenact that scene for me."

I lean in for a kiss, much to the delight of his friends, who are now whooping and cheering us on.

"Take me to bed or lose me forever," I say, keeping with the *Top Gun* theme. I cringe for just a moment, realizing Ken and I also shared some sexy time involving this movie. At least we're in very different scenes.

Before I can dwell too long on it, Peter has scooped me up in his arms and is walking me triumphantly to the door.

We immediately excuse ourselves from his friends back at the apartment and head to his room for some alone time. I'm still torn about my slow down rule and wonder again if I'll be able to resist sleeping with him tonight. We've both been drinking, but we're not nearly as drunk as we were the last time we were in this room. I decide to just see where the night takes us and enjoy whatever happens.

Peter's strong arms are cradling me as we kiss in his bed, and I'm so content I know I won't mind if this is all we do. His friends are in the middle of some loud video game and it's a bit distracting anyway; I'm not sure I'd like our first time to be set with that kind of background noise.

"Are they going to play all night?" I ask, pulling away for just a minute.

"Probably," he says. "Want me to turn on some music and we can get some sleep?"

"Actually, that sounds perfect." It's the truth. Peter is on board with the whole Prom Night Plan and being a perfect gentleman about it. It's refreshing. He turns on some classical music and climbs back in bed with me. It isn't long before we're both asleep.

I must have had a crazy dream last night, because not only am I smiling when I wake up in his arms, but I'm feeling a little naughty. I think it was something about being in the backseat of his car again, but now there's no one to walk in on us, I decide to see if I can start the morning off with some fun. I kiss Peter gently on the cheek, but he doesn't stir, clearly a heavy sleeper like I am. Knowing the best way to wake a guy up is with a bit more than kissing, I reach my hand down between his legs to see if he was also having any dreams.

Not only was he not having dreams like that, but I'm confused by what I find. I thought when we were fooling around before that Peter's dick just wasn't hard from drinking, which I totally get. But as I reach my hand inside his boxers, I realize that, even hard, this is the smallest dick I've ever come in contact with. It might actually be hard right now, I realize, and nearly gasp.

Okay. Calm down. This is not a big deal. But my hand is still inside his boxers and he's starting to wake up. I pull my hand out abruptly and accidentally smack myself in the face. The sound is enough to startle Peter into opening his eyes and I jump up out of bed.

"Everything okay?" he says. "Come back to bed."

"I totally forgot," I say, a little too quickly. "I have to be somewhere this morning."

"Where?" he asks groggily.

Anywhere away from your pencil dick, I think, trying to come up with a better answer. But now the image of one of those tiny golf score pencils is in my head and that's exactly what it felt like and oh my God I have to get out of here.

"Golf," I say. "I have a tee time this morning with my instructor."

"I'll walk you to your car." He starts to get up.

"No, no. Don't be silly." I hold my hands up as if to keep him and the world's smallest penis in bed. "I'll text you later today. Get some more sleep."

I lean in to kiss him goodbye, then bounce out of the room as quickly as possible. In the early light of morning, though, I realize pretty quickly that I am lost. Not figuratively, as I have been a lot this year, but really and truly lost. I have no idea where I parked my car last night and every building looks exactly the same in this place. I'm not sure I could even find Peter's apartment again on my own, having never walked there by myself.

This would have been a great distraction from thinking about what I'd just discovered, except for one inconvenient fact: I have to pee. And not just a little bit. I haven't gone to the bathroom this morning and have a full bladder that I need to empty in a hurry.

As I turn a corner in the complex on my now frantic search for my car, the sprinklers turn on at the patch of grass to my right. I'm struggling to hold this crazy amount of pee inside my body when a brilliant-yet-gross thought jumps into my mind: *pee in the grass.*

I don't even take the time to weigh the pros and cons before looking around to make sure the coast is clear, then striding confidently into the grass and just letting go. I'm wearing a skirt and flip-flops and soon my legs are soaking wet with urine and sprinkler water, but I couldn't have cared less. The relief is so instant that nothing could have bothered me in this moment.

I walk slowly through the sprinklers, hoping to pass it off as a casual, nostalgic stroll in case anyone comes by, but I am soon nearly the end of the grass and not quite done peeing yet. I turn about ninety degrees to extend my walk so I can completely finish when I hear it. Laughter.

I'm pretty sure the laughter is coming from the building behind me, so I walk swiftly to the building in front of me, finally now done watering the grass. As I approach that building, the laughter gets louder, and I realize the empty patio I am now walking toward is anything but empty. Smiling up at me from a chair on the deck is a cute, dark-haired guy with glasses. And unless my luck has suddenly improved, it's definitely the guy who I hit in the head with my shoe a week ago.

"Lovely day for a sprinkle," he says, his voice giving away a British accent I hadn't noticed before.

"I, er, yes," I say. "I was just looking for my car and the water came on as I crossed the grass…"

"Sure, sure. Happens to me all the time. And then I think to myself *you're in* trouble now."

Did he just say "you're in" trouble because it sounds like urine? Did he see me pee? Am I being paranoid?

I laugh awkwardly and turn back toward the parking lot, hoping to God our interaction is over. But as I go to leave, my shoe sticks in the muddy grass and I have to backtrack to get it. Why am I always doing terribly embarrassing things and losing shoes around this guy?

I hear him laugh a bit again as I scurry away and keep my car search confined to the pavement going forward. I finally find my car and climb in, wet, embarrassed, and kinda smelly. I'm looking forward to taking a shower, but don't think I can wash away the icky feelings that are now hanging all over me. I guess it's worth a try.

Chapter Thirty-Two

March 22

I'm having dinner with Meg tonight, hoping she can help me get my head on straight after P Day (referring, of course, to both peeing in the grass and discovering Peter's small…peter).

"How small is it?" she asks, for about the tenth time since we've sat down.

I hold up my pinky to give her a visual and she tries not to react, but I can see my own expression reflected in hers.

"We'd be so pissed if a guy rejected us over something physical," I say, an argument that I've been having with myself over and over. "Like, remember when Ricky said I had small boobs back in seventh grade and that's why he didn't want to go to the dance with me?"

"He said you had *no* boobs and he said it in front of our entire math class." She's clearly still just as pissed about it as I am. "But that's different."

"Is it? How is not wanting to be with Peter because he has a small dick any different?"

"Sex is important in a relationship," she points out, just as I've also been telling myself all week. "If he's not able to have sex with you, I feel like you'd be really missing out. Is he willing to talk about options?"

"We've been going out for three weeks! I don't even know his middle name. How can I ask him something like that? And wait—there are options for something like this?"

"I don't know. You're not even sure he can get it up. Maybe a little Viagra would be a good start."

I nod, thoughtfully. If Viagra can help men have sex way past their prime, maybe it would help this guy who's still in his. It's the first bit of hope I've had.

"We're supposed to have sex after the Prom." I wince at the thought. "It's going to be just like high school where the guy puts it in and you're not sure what's happening and ack—I can't do this."

I shudder at the thought of trying to sleep with Peter and can't decide if I'm mad at myself or just sad over the situation.

"This is ridiculous," I say, suddenly finding a new fortitude. "We are really hitting it off and I haven't even attempted sex with him yet.

Who's to say he doesn't totally make it work just fine? He has to be aware of his…shortcomings. Maybe I'm worrying over nothing."

"There's the spirit," says Meg, cheering me on. "Now let's talk dresses. What are you wearing to the Prom?"

We chat for about an hour about my style choices for the evening, flipping through the pictures I've brought with me of all the dresses that are in the running. It's just like sitting at the cafeteria in high school and I'm suddenly especially sad that Kim isn't there for it. She was with me when I picked my other prom dresses, and we were all there for Meg's wedding dress appointments. I wonder what she'd do if I texted her the options?

While Meg excuses herself to use the restroom, I do just that.

> ***Me:*** *Which do you think I should wear to the Prom next week? Can't decide and you've always been better at this than me.*

I assume I won't hear back soon or at all, so I'm surprised when my phone vibrates in my hand with her quick reply.

> ***Kim:*** *The blue one. They're all lovely, but I think the blue one is best. Just not the red one. Trust me.*

I am so excited to hear from her that I don't quite notice the weird tone of her text right away. I send a response (*Thanks! Miss you!*), then show Meg, who has come back to the table, looking at my excited face with curiosity.

"I'm going with the blue dress," I say. "And Kim helped me pick!"

"That's great!" she says. "And I agree. I was thinking that or the red one."

"She said definitely not to the red one. Not sure why, but she's always had the best taste of the three of us."

"Agreed. So glad to hear you two are talking again."

It's just a quick text exchange over a fashion decision, but I can't help but agree. Kim would also probably have great advice on the PD discussion, but I decide to leave it at dresses for now.

Chapter Thirty-Three

March 23

I'm at the tuxedo rental shop with Peter, and I must say: he looks pretty damn fine all dressed up. I'm going to have the cutest date at the Prom!

"Do you think this looks too good?" he says, smirking as he walks out of the dressing room. "I'd hate to show you up."

"Oh, don't you worry," I say. "With the dress I'm going to wear, I think we'll both be turning some heads next week."

"What color is your dress?" the woman who works at the shop asks me. "I've got vests and pocket squares we can choose from to co-ordinate the whole look."

"It's blue," I reply. "That would be great if you can bring out the selection. I'll see which one is closest."

"Blue?" Peter sounds a bit disappointed. "I thought you might wear red like you did back in high school at that one dance."

I am genuinely shocked he remembers that, but I did wear a red dress to the Winter Formal one year that was especially pretty. It really makes me feel special that he noticed me so much all those years ago and can still recall such specific details.

"Well," I say, "I did have a red dress in the running, but I thought I'd go with a different one. But you know what? I could go with the red if it means so much to you."

He smiles and pulls me in for a quick kiss before heading back into the dressing room to change. I pick out a few accessories for him that will look great with my dress, and we finish up at the shop.

"Do you have time to hang a bit longer?" I ask. "Or do you have to get back to the gym?"

"I'm all yours," he says. "What did you have in mind?"

"I thought we could go back to my place and hang out for a bit." I raise my eyebrows in a meaningful way.

He nods excitedly and we hop in my car to make the short drive to my condo. I have a renewed sense of determination where the physical part of our relationship is concerned and have decided to test some of my theories today. First of all, how sure can I be that there even is a problem when I've barely been able to assess Peter's situation? Maybe he's got really great mind control and is taking my Prom plan super seriously. I read something online saying that some men who practice tantric sex are able to avoid an erection until they are really ready to do the deed. Maybe Peter does that and keeps himself small until he basically turns into the Hulk or something?

Okay, that doesn't sound like a real thing, but still, no need to panic until I can do more reconnaissance.

We walk into my living room holding hands and sink down on the couch together with me now sitting on his lap. I feel so dainty in his arms it almost makes me laugh. How can this strong, sexy guy be someone I'm worried about performing well in bed?

We start to kiss and before I know it, we are rounding first base well on our way to second. Or maybe we've rounded second and we're on our way to third. I've never actually known which base is which, other than a home run is clearly doing it.

Baseball analogies aside, Peter is now removing my bra and laying me back onto the couch. He begins to unbutton my pants, then pauses for a second.

"Did you still want to wait until next week?" he says.

"Eh." I shrug. "We've waited long enough."

"If you're sure." He continues with the undressing.

"I'm sure," I say, laughing at how eager his hands are moving. I know he'd wait if I asked him to, but he most definitely wants to keep going.

I'm naked and smiling up at Peter as he quickly removes all his clothing. He must be sure of himself to take everything off so quickly and I barely have a chance to glance at what's going on between his legs when he lies down on top of me and kisses me full on.

"Hmm," he says, sliding himself between my legs. "I've wanted this for so long."

"Me, too," I say. "I can't wait to feel you inside me."

"Oh, you want more?" He thrusts our hips bones back together.

"I want everything you've got." I reach my arms around him to pull him closer to me.

He's thrusting back and forth now and I'm still waiting to feel him enter me when I realize he already has. We're having sex right now and I can barely feel anything. I thought he was still teasing me with a little pre-sex warm-up, but I can now kinda feel something like the tip of a normal, albeit skinny, penis inside me. I've barely registered its presence when Peter starts to make a familiar face and I realize he's just about done. Or wait, I guess he's done.

"Yes," he says, sighing and collapsing on top of me. "Did you finish?"

"Did I finish?" I do my best not to sound incredulous.

"Yeah. I've been told I'm pretty good at taking care of my ladies. Did you come?"

"Uh, no."

"Oh, is that hard for you to do?" He genuinely sounds concerned.

"Uh, er, I guess?" I truly do not want to go into detail with a guy who is seriously clueless about the female orgasm.

And who are these women who have been telling him he's good in bed? I want to tell them all off, one by one. How dare they send this poor man out into the world thinking he can just poke his tiny penis around for a minute and that will be enough to bring a girl to climax. I can't be mad at Peter. Okay, I kinda can, because he's old enough to not be so damn clueless, but these other women? They share some of the blame here.

I'm really starting to get amped up when Peter jumps up to take a shower. I'm planning to have some diagrams and visual aids ready for when he comes back out until I realize that it might be more fun to teach him on a real-life model, i.e., me.

I follow him to my bathroom and join him in the shower. I picture myself as Monica Gellar showing Chandler Bing how to get a woman off, smiling as I picture her shouting the word "seven" over and over again. Whether I end up marrying this guy or not, I will not let him unleash that tiny pecker onto another vagina without doing some work.

"Hey there," he says. "Did you want to go again? Cuz I could probably be ready here in another minute."

"Actually," I say, "I'm not quite done with round one yet."

"Huh?" He looks at me with such honest bewilderment that I know I'm going to have my work cut out.

"I didn't orgasm, and any woman who says she has with you is lying if that's how you normally operate."

I brace myself for a defensive reply, but I'm happy to see he at least seems open to this discussion.

"Well, I usually do a bit more," he says. "But I just couldn't wait to have you."

Okay, this is encouraging. Again, I was judging him unfairly. The guy can't change his body, but maybe I missed out on some sort of legendary foreplay.

"Show me," I say. "We'll call it Round One point five."

Peter closes the gap between us and kisses me passionately. An excellent start. He begins fondling my chest like he did in the car the other night, and I mentally give him a B+ for hand technique.

"That do anything for you?" he says into my ear.

"Keep going," I say.

He slides his right hand off my chest and moves it down between my legs. Apparently unaware that the clitoris is a thing, he quickly puts two fingers inside me. Seeing as how this is about a thousand times bigger than his penis, though, it's a nice feeling. He's still going strong with his digits while he moves his mouth, which had been kissing my neck, down to my breasts.

I moan a bit to encourage him when he suddenly stops and stands back upright to kiss me.

"There you go," he says, turning back to finish his shower. "Told you I could take care of you."

Oh. My. God. He thinks that moan was an orgasm. He thinks any time a woman makes noise during sex she is in the throes of passion. He has watched too much porn. Or Cinemax at night. Or has skated by on his looks for so long that no woman was ever brave enough to tell him he is terrible in bed.

I've already challenged him on this issue once today and decide I don't have the patience to try again, so I step out of the shower and decide to call in reinforcements. I quietly grab the vibrator out of the drawer by my bed and sneak into the kitchen to get myself off. It doesn't take me long to get there, but I don't have a chance to put my vibrator back in my room before Peter strides into the kitchen wearing nothing but a towel, so I throw it into a cabinet under the sink.

"Can we go to one of your shops to get some ice cream?" he asks. "Sex always makes me hungry."

"Sure," I say. Now that I've taken care of myself, a scoop or two of ice cream does sound pretty great. And besides, I have no desire to think about this predicament a moment longer. Ice cream will be the perfect distraction.

Chapter Thirty-Four

www.flavorsofthemonth.bloggerific.com

It's only four days to the Prom—do you have your tickets? Don't forget: Sinfully Good will be there dishing out dessert! Ice cream and supporting a good cause. What could be better?

This month has been a big lesson for me in both who I was and who I want to be. I have realized on more than one occasion that I should have spoken up in high school about how I felt. And with that realization has come the extra confidence I need to speak up about things I want in my life right now. It's getting late in the month, and I still don't have an April flavor lined up, so let me say this publicly in case any potential dates are reading this: I want to be swept off my feet. Maybe it's the

Prom coming up or maybe I've just watched too many romantic comedies, but I am in the mood for a Prince Charming situation, and I don't care how silly that sounds.

So, if you've got a ton of romance coursing through your body that you're ready to put out into the world, let's see if we can have a fairy-tale ending, shall we?

MARCH 27

It's finally here—Prom night! I've spent the day getting pampered and feel like the prettiest girl in the world when Peter knocks on my door. He's wearing the tux we picked out and carrying a dozen red roses and I nearly cry as he walks through my door. This is just how I pictured it in high school and it's almost too perfect for words.

We're not compatible sexually, though, says a little voice inside my head. I keep telling her to shut up, but she keeps coming back. I am comforted by the fact that Peter genuinely seems interested in pleasing me, but it will take more than one lesson in the shower to catch him up on the ins and outs of female sexuality. I haven't given up, but I'm no longer expecting tonight to end with the perfect sex I was hoping for.

"You look amazing," he says, taking in my whole look from head to toe. "It's just like that dress you wore to Prom."

"Winter Formal," I say, not sure why I'm correcting him.

"That can't be right," he says, making a face. "I didn't go to Winter Formal. I mean the dress you wore to prom with that kid from the plays. The gay kid. I thought he was so lucky getting to dance with you all night when he didn't even like girls."

He's laughing now at the memory, and I am fully confused. I did go to Winter Formal with a friend of mine who everyone thought was gay, but after he tried to have sex with me in front of my parents' house that night, I was pretty sure he liked girls just fine.

I'm still confused by Peter's comments but soon forget all about questionably gay former dates as I take in how my current prom date looks standing in my kitchen. He's incredibly handsome and sweet. I cross over to him to kiss him when he puts a hand up to stop me.

"Before I kiss you, I have a surprise for you," he says with a big smile on his face.

"What's that?" I look around to see if he was holding something other than the roses. I don't see anything, but he crosses to me before I can evaluate if he's got something in his pocket. He scoops me up into his arms and marches me back to the bedroom before I can protest about messing up my perfectly coiffed hair.

He sets me gently down on the bed and stands to face me.

"I have been doing some research and think I can do better on that whole orgasm thing," he says, so proud of himself that I almost want to laugh.

"Oh yeah?"

"Yes." He nods. "I'm not suggesting that we have sex before we go, but I wanted to give you a little preview."

"A little preview sounds delightful," I say, wondering what he could have learned in a couple of days and definitely in the mood to find out.

"For a proper preview, I'm going to have to ask that you remove your dress."

As there's no way I'd be able to pull the skirt of my dress up to my hips, I'm inclined to agree. I turn around so he can unzip me and gently place my beautiful dress on the side of the bed. I walk back to Peter and sit back down on the bed. Peter gently pulls my panties down and sets them aside. He then takes a second before gently spreading my legs apart and I hear him fiddling with something on his lap.

Before I can ask what he's doing, he begins gently caressing my inner thighs with his hands and brings his face between my legs to kiss me softly. It's such an improvement from our previous attempts at anything that I'm super impressed, but I decide to see what else he can do before offering any comments.

Soon, he is using his tongue to find my clitoris and I'm so surprised that I say, "Yes! Good job!" before I can help myself.

"There's more where that came from," he says, taking another second with whatever is on his lap before getting back to the work at hand.

All in all, it's pretty decent head. He seems unsure of himself, but he's got a good rhythm going. I don't quite orgasm, but it's getting late and I want him to be proud of himself, so I let out a shudder and some energetic moans to signal that he can stop.

"Did I do it?" he says, sounding like a high school kid looking for praise from a teacher.

"That was great," I say, standing up and pulling him up to kiss me. And I genuinely mean it. I may not have finished, but I definitely could have gotten there with a bit of coaching and if I wasn't so worried about messing up my hair. It's hard to focus on oral pleasure when you're trying not to move too much.

I look down to the ground to search for my underwear when I see a small piece of paper between us.

"Oh," Peter says bashfully, scooping it up. "I, uh, brought some notes."

He literally has a diagram showing him where to find the clit and it's so cute I can hardly stand it. Anyone this eager to learn is just fine by me.

"This is one test where cheating is encouraged," I say with a laugh.

Peter helps me back into my dress and we head out for the Prom. I'm walking with a bit of a spring in my step, feeling for the first time this month that I can officially add a third name to my list of potential husbands.

*

Peter and I walk up the grand staircase at the Wrigley Mansion on our way to the Prom, and I cannot stop smiling. I'm so glad he told me to wear this red dress as I feel every eye turn toward us on the way in. I'm relatively well-known at these events, so a little attention isn't abnormal, but something about the combination of how I look tonight and the handsome man on my arm is causing quite a stir.

"Everyone here is staring at us," Peter says, also delighting a bit in all the attention. "Must be because I've got the prettiest date here. Care to dance?"

The dance floor is empty because it's so early, but I let Peter spin me around and do a little swaying before we cross to the back of the room. Samantha arrived earlier to set up our table and I smile as I lean in to give her a hug. She's smiling, too, but I see the hint of a weird look on her face as she comes close to whisper in my ear.

"Don't panic," she says.

"About what?" I say, instinctively panicking.

"Kim's here and she's walking this way and she's wearing the exact same dress you are wearing," she blurts out in one breath.

I turn around to see it's true. Kim, who is inexplicably here, despite not having told me she'd be attending, is wearing the same dress I am and we look like the friggin' Bobbsey Twins.

Peter is standing between us smiling awkwardly and trying to defuse the situation with a friendly introduction.

"Hi," he says, reaching out to shake her hand. "I'm Peter and this is Cynthia. You might not realize it, but you two apparently have very similar taste in fashion."

I want to kiss him. Sure, his little attempt at levity has done nothing to ease the crinkle in Kim's brow, but he's trying and that's what matters.

"Actually," I say, "this is Kim and she's a good friend of mine."

"Who specifically told you not to wear that dress," is Kim's curt response.

"But who didn't say why," I fire back. "Seriously, I never would have worn this if I'd known you'd be here in the same thing. Why didn't you just tell me?"

"It's a beautiful night." Kim relaxes her face a bit. "Why don't I spend the evening on the patio while you do your thing in here?"

"You just want to avoid me all night?" I no longer care that we're in the same dress at all. I just want my friend back.

"We look ridiculous. And besides, I know you're always busy at these events. We'll catch up later."

And with that, she turns to walk away, not turning back once to see that I'm standing there trying not to cry. We've been at the Prom for five minutes and I've already caused a scene and nearly cried. It's fitting, really.

"I'll go get us a couple drinks," says Peter, leaving me with Sam.

"Well, that's one thing that adult Prom has over original Prom," I say with a sigh. "Booze."

"My Prom had alcohol," says Sam, challenging me.

"Yeah, but you had to sneak it in," I say with a laugh.

"True," she says. "And I'm pretty sure all we had was Boone's Farm. That stuff is nasty when you're throwing it up the next morning."

We both burst into laughter, trading stories about the worst hangovers we had as kids. I soon forget, or at least stop obsessing, about Kim and the dress debacle. Sam's date is a guy named Jason, and he and Peter are chatting about the best way to strengthen your biceps or something or other while Sam and I chat with other business owners about the weather, local sports, and other basic small talk topics. A few of them ask how my husband hunt is going, with some of the ladies I've known for a while eyeing Peter with excited eyes.

"Can I have him if you don't want him?" one of them asks, too tipsy to realize it's a bit of an absurd question.

Before I can answer, Peter steps in between us, rescuing me from an awkward conversation.

"Excuse me, ladies, but I've been neglecting my date," he says, taking my hand and walking me to the dance floor.

"My hero," I say, as we start to sway to the music.

We're toward the middle of the song when Peter pulls his face back to look me in the eye.

"Can I ask you something?" he says in a serious tone.

"I think you just did. But feel free to ask another."

"Why did you never respond to my letter?"

"What letter?" I'm confused and curious.

"I handed you a letter on my last day of high school," he says earnestly. "I came and found you in your French class and gave it to you."

"I didn't take French." My heart starts racing.

"Yes, you did," he continues. "You had French right next to my history class. I saw you there every day, but never knew your name. It took me all year to get up the courage to write you that letter. I put my phone number in it and asked you to call me, but you never did."

I realize with a jolt why so many things haven't added up this month.

"Cara." I put my hands over my mouth. "You had a crush on Cara."

How did I not realize this sooner? A lot of people confused me with Cara through the years. Cara, who was the lead in the school musicals. Cara, who moved to our school from California in the middle of Freshman year and wore LA Dodgers hats all the time. Cara, who must have worn a red dress to the prom with one of the guys she did all those plays with. Cara, who looked a lot like me, but had the boobs so many guys dreamed of seeing in high school, including Peter.

"No, no." Peter shakes his head, but I can see the light of recognition start to creep onto his face. Or rather, the light of non-recognition, as he looks at me closely and realizes I am not the girl he'd seen every day going into French class. I took Spanish on the other side of campus, and always felt invisible when I'd seen Peter in the quad or in the cafeteria. Apparently, that's exactly what I'd been.

"You're not her." He becomes rigid in my arms. "Why didn't you tell me?"

"I didn't know you thought I was her," I protest, very annoyed that this is turning out to be my fault.

"You had to have known on some level," he snaps. "You didn't even wear a red dress to prom, did you?"

"I told you I didn't." I now wish we were having this conversation anywhere but a crowded dance floor.

"I can't believe you lied to me." He puts his hands by his side and takes a step away from me. "And after all I did to try and please you in bed."

Now I'm trying not to laugh, cry, and maybe slap him for being such a jerk, but all I can do is say, "Want me to give you her phone number?"

Peter's eyes light up and I know I've found the best way to stop this whole thing from turning into an embarrassing scene. "Do you have it? Is she single?"

"I think so," I say, honestly not sure of her relationship status other than what I've seen on Facebook. We were never close in school, but I'm pretty sure I have her contact information from the last reunion. She was always nice, and we liked to trade stories about people confusing us for each other. Now we might just have the greatest/worst of those stories to laugh about ever.

We walk off the dance floor and I grab my phone from the purse I've left with Samantha. She's giving me a questioning look, having picked up on the very different vibe surrounding Peter and me post-dance.

"I'll tell you later," I say, rolling my eyes.

I text Peter the number I have for Cara from my phone.

"Thanks," he says. "I'm not sure what to say. I really enjoyed getting to know you this month, but if there's any chance that Cara and I could work out..."

"You've gotta at least give it a try," I say, finishing his sentence.

I'm sad but honestly don't want to be with a guy who would always be dreaming about someone else. Besides, I think to myself with a chuckle, maybe Cara can take over as Peter's new sex coach. And anyway, she dated enough closeted gay guys in high school and college that she might not even care too much if he's bad in bed.

"Good luck with your search," he says, kissing me on the cheek.

"You're not going to stay for the rest of the dance?" I ask.

"I think I'm going to call Cara." He's clearly too focused on that to be much of a date anymore anyway.

"Yeah. I guess that makes sense. See ya around."

"See ya." He turns to leave.

"You show up to the Prom wearing the same dress as your friend," says Sam, coming up behind me to provide a recap of the evening.

"Yup," I say.

"And your date leaves you to go call some other girl midway through the evening," she adds.

"Yup," I sigh.

"And we're all out of Mint Chocolate Chip," she says.

"What?" I spin around to face her. "That's the worst part!"

We're both cracking up again, but I really could go for a scoop of that flavor. I'm feeling a bit low and it always cheers me up. I instead settle for Cookie Crush Supreme, the flavor I made with Peter in mind. It's delicious, but a bit messy, and I spill a few drops on my dress.

"Perfect," I say under my breath. "Par for the course of this wonderful evening."

As I walk to the bathroom to try to clean myself up, I look out on the patio as I pass it. And there, across the courtyard, I see Kim. More importantly, I see Kim's date. She hasn't been avoiding me all night because of the dress thing. She's been avoiding me so I won't see her date.

It's Javier.

*

I turn before I can be sure if Javier has seen me and decide to make a break for it. After everything that's happened tonight, I cannot handle any more drama and deciphering what the hell it means for Kim and Javier to be together might be the craziest thing in a string of absurdity tonight. I'm walking as fast as I can when I suddenly decide it's not quite enough and I break into a run.

The funny thing about running in an evening gown and heels is you basically can't do it. I'm about halfway down the entrance steps when my foot touches concrete and I realize I've accidentally stepped out of one of my Jimmy Choos. It's almost enough to make me lose my balance, but I luckily just come to an awkward stop as I turn around to see my shoe falling down the rest of the steps without me.

The shoe comes to a stop in front of a man who bends down to pick it up.

"Sorry," I call down to him. "Just call me Cinderella."

"Only if you'll call me Prince Charming," says a voice I'm sure I've heard somewhere before.

I pull off my other shoe, as I'm completely unable to navigate the stairs with one shoe on and one shoe off, and hurry down to see that the man holding my shoe is none other than Peter's downstairs neighbor. I'm immediately bummed that this isn't my first time meeting him because there is literally no cuter way to meet a guy than having him find your shoe as you are running away from a ball, but I'm also quickly beaming from ear to ear. This guy is really cute. And he made a Cinderella joke.

"I believe this belongs to you," he says, holding out my shoe for me.

Oh yeah. He's also British, I remember, suddenly lost in his accent.

"What are you doing here?" I say.

"I'm here to see you." He gives me a sheepish grin. "I, uh, asked Peter about you and found your blog. Based on your previous escape attempts from his apartment, I figured things weren't going all that well and thought, maybe, you might like to meet a real prince."

"You're a prince?" I'm shocked and giddy at the thought.

"Eric Prince." He offers his hand to introduce himself. "Not officially royal, but your blog didn't specify that you needed a Windsor or anything, so I thought I might be close enough. If it helps, I once visited Buckingham Palace on a field trip."

"Did you meet the Queen?" I joke.

"Of course. She was lovely. We played Nintendo together for hours."

He's witty. And handsome. And he came here for me. This night might just be turning around.

"As you already seemed to be running away, shall we get out of here and chat more about how wonderful we both are?"

I remember why I was trying to leave abruptly and turn to see if anyone followed me out of the Prom. Everything looks clear, though, and I can think of no good reason to stay here a minute longer.

"That sounds perfect," I say, taking the arm he's offering me after putting my shoes back on.

We walk toward the valet stand, and I chuckle to myself, realizing how weird it is to be leaving with a different date than I walked in with.

"You're one confident dude," I say, appraising Eric again with fresh eyes. "Walking into an event where I've got a date and trying to steal me away."

"Actually," he admits, "I was just going to ask you for a dance and see if you'd found anyone for April yet. But this worked out even better."

"Ah, that makes way more sense," I say with a smile. "You just got lucky that I had such a bad night."

"What would make your night better?" he asks.

"Honestly, you've already saved the day. I'm not sure what you could possibly do to make things any better."

"Hmm. I might have an idea. Any chance you're up for a spontaneous road trip?"

"Can I go home and change first? I spilled some ice cream on my dress."

"Okay," he laughs. "But otherwise our attire would be perfect."

As the valet brings his car around, I suddenly realize I've just agreed to go on a road trip with a stranger. It's not my most adult decision ever, but I'm still in high school brain mode and apparently making decisions like a seventeen-year-old.

"You're not a serial killer or anything, are you?" I ask, deciding to do some due diligence.

"How many people do you have to kill to reach serial status?" he says, again with the perfect combination of snark and British accent.

We stop by my house so I can change and pack a quick bag, then stop by his apartment so he can do the same. I stay in the car at his place to make sure I don't see Peter or any of his friends, and it's just a few minutes before we hit the road. I decide I'd better send a quick text to Meg so someone knows where I am and who I'm with.

> ***Me:*** *Heading on a spontaneous road trip with Eric Prince. He lives in the apartment below Peter. Prom was a disaster, but I'll explain later.*
>
> ***Meg:*** *Wait—what? Where are you going?*
>
> ***Me:*** *We're heading west on the I-10. I'll send you a text when we get where we're going.*

My phone dings again as Eric and I trade a few get-to-know-you questions, but I don't bother checking it. If I let Meg's questions enter my brain, I may call this whole thing off, and I just want to be anywhere but home right now. It's been an absolutely crazy first quarter of the year and I want nothing more than to clear my head while getting to know the guy sitting next to me.

At least, I was planning to talk with him during the long car ride, but I wake up the next morning when Eric is talking to a parking lot attendant.

"Where are we?" I say, stretching my arms and legs and trying to rub the crick in my neck out from sleeping at a weird angle.

"Well," he says, "you seemed sad, so I thought I'd take you to the Happiest Place on Earth."

"*What*?" I sit up so quickly that I nearly make myself lightheaded.

I take in our surroundings and realize he has driven us to Disneyland. My favorite place on the planet. I left a Ball last night with a guy named Prince and he's taken me to a castle.

I look over at Eric who is beaming from ear to ear, clearly pleased with himself for pulling off this surprise. It's not even officially his month yet and I'm already in the middle of a fairytale.

Holy. Fucking. Shit.

Acknowledgements

When I started writing this book eight years ago, I thought it would be so easy. And in many ways, the writing was. But everything that came after the writing? Not so much. This story wouldn't be out in the world if not for my team of friends and family who wouldn't let me give up on my publishing dream. Brittany and Nicci—your constant encouragement and feedback through the years has meant the world to me. My other two early readers, Mom and Candy—I know it can't always have been easy to read the sexy scenes, but your open minds and support helped keep me going. Mark—I like you and I love you. Anna, Paul, Lucy—I hope you don't read this for a long time, but all of my dreams came true the days you were born and I will never be able to adequately tell you how much I adore you.

To my team at NineStar—thank you for loving my books enough to pick them up and guide me through this process. Elizabeth—you are a patient and talented editor. I'm so lucky to have you on my team.

And to everyone who read the early iterations of this story and waited years for the conclusion—thank you for hanging in there with me. I hope you are excited to see where this story goes. To readers just now finding this story—welcome! Enjoy! Settle for nothing less than a love that lights you up inside.

About Penny McLean

Penny McLean is a careerwoman by day, writer by night, mother at all times to three incredible children, and wife to a loving husband. Born in San Diego, California, she now hails from Gilbert, Arizona where she especially enjoys giving back to her community by volunteering at schools and libraries, with Girl Scouts, and for any causes that benefit marginalized communities, especially LGBTQIA+ youth. She began her career as a writer at the age of 17 when she was hired to cover movies, arts, and features for a youth-oriented page in the *Arizona Republic*. With twenty years of writing experience for magazines, newspapers, social media, and more, she is thrilled to have her first novel out in the world.

Website

www.nerdygirlapproved.com

Coming Soon from Penny McLean

The Predicament

Flavors of the Month, Book Two

It's weird to be in such a familiar place with a complete stranger. I know every twist and turn of Disneyland, but when I look at the guy walking next to me, I keep realizing again what a strange path I've been on this year.

"So, you dated Peter as part of your Plan?" Eric asks, as I finish explaining everything that's happened since I set this all in motion in December.

I nod. "But we met back in high school. I had a huge crush on him back in the day and he thought he had one on me."

"But he really liked that Cara girl?"

"Apparently," I say sheepishly. "People used to confuse us from time to time, but this has to be the worst instance of mistaken identity I've ever experienced."

"I'll say. I once had a girl throw eggs at my door back in London. When I yelled down to ask what she was doing, she said she meant to hit my neighbor's house, but got the number wrong. It was annoying. Yours is worse."

I laugh really hard and smile at Eric as we stroll down Main Street toward Sleeping Beauty's Castle. It's crowded today and we've already had to dodge a few strollers being pushed by frantic parents, eager to maximize their children's happiness for the day. It looks exhausting.

We stop for a minute to sit on a bench and watch the people passing by. Or rather, Eric is watching the other people, while I'm taking the opportunity to stare at him and assess his looks. It's shallow, but I don't care.

The verdict? He is really, really cute. The glasses I noticed the first time I saw him currently sit slightly askew on his face, or they do until he reaches up to adjust them. His black hair is unkempt, most likely because we drove all night to get here. His eyes are a steely gray and his build is tall and lanky.

"Why did you bring me here?" I say as the thought occurs to me. "Don't get me wrong; I'm thrilled. But what put it in your head to get in the car and drive straight here?"

"Well, I haven't lived in America very long, but I did a lot of touristy things pretty early. I came here last year with a coworker while we were visiting a lab in Los Angeles and I thought how nice it would be to come back with a woman on a date. So, when I saw you looking like you needed an escape last night, I decided this would be the best option."

"And you went to the Prom last night just to see me?" I'm still a bit mystified.

"Indeed I did. Something about seeing your legs dangle outside of my tree that night really left an impression."

We're both laughing again, but I'm secretly wondering if he's holding back regarding our second encounter. I decide not to mention it and opt for the best distraction I can think of.

Connect with NineStar Press

WWW.NINESTARPRESS.COM

WWW.FACEBOOK.COM/NINESTARPRESS

WWW.FACEBOOK.COM/GROUPS/NINESTARNICHE

WWW.TWITTER.COM/NINESTARPRESS

WWW.INSTAGRAM.COM/NINESTARPRESS

Printed in the USA
CPSIA information can be obtained
at www.ICGtesting.com
LVHW020209060923
757155LV00004B/77